Broken Whispers

PERFECTLY IMPERFECT SERIES

NEVA ALTAJ

Editing by Susan Stradiotto (www.susanstradiotto.com)
Proofreading #1 by Beyond The Proof (www.beyondtheproof.ca)
Proofreading #2 by Proofreading By Mich (@proofreadingbymich)
Cover design by Deranged Doctor (www.derangeddoctordesign.com)

Author's Note

American Sign Language (ASL) is used frequently in this book for communication. While the sentence structure of the ASL is considerably different from spoken language, I took the creative liberty to have the ASL dialogue follow the American English grammar rules for an easier story flow. I hope you won't mind this decision.

There are a few Russian words mentioned in the book, so here are the translations and clarifications:

Solnyshko—***солнышко*** (little sun; sunshine); used as endearment.

Zayka—***зайка*** (bunny); used as endearment.

Lenochka—a diminutive form of Lena.

Piroshki—***пирожки*** (hand pies); these are small pastries that could be made savory (filled with minced meat and/or vegetables) or sweet (filled with fruit or jams) and can be either baked or fried.

Dusha moya—душа моя (my soul, soul mate); used as endearment

"Ya lyublyu tebya vsey dushoy, solnyshko . . . Ya ne pozvolyu nikomu zabrat' tebya".—"I love you with all my heart, sunshine . . . I won't let anyone take you away."

"Ty luch solntsa v pasmurnyy den'"—"You are a ray of light in a cloudy day."

Trigger warning:

Please be aware that this book contains content that may trigger certain audiences: domestic violence, mentions of abuse, and graphic descriptions of violence and torture (none occur between the hero/heroine).

BROKEN whispers

prologue

Mikhail

Twelve years ago

A DOOR BURSTING OPEN PIERCES THROUGH MY hazy consciousness, followed by the sense of falling in slow motion. Unfamiliar voices whisper somewhere far away, gradually becoming louder, until all I can hear is hurried shouting.

A gasp to my left, "Dear God."

I try opening my eyes but fail. It takes me a few tries before I manage to peel my eyelids apart, but all I can see are blurry shapes.

And then comes the pain.

It feels like I've been stabbed by a thousand knives, with the blades remaining lodged in my flesh. The sharp, searing, body-wide sensation encompasses everything.

I choke on my breath and try to talk, but the only thing that comes out is a pained wheezing gasp. The void closes in again, the sounds slowly fade, and I let myself float away. The last thing I remember are broken sentences that breach my fading consciousness until there is nothing left. Only the pain.

"Roman! . . . Mikhail is still alive!"

"Jesus . . . press something over his face . . ."

"I'm not sure he'll make it . . ."

"Anyone else?"

"No, they're all dead."

Chapter *one*

Mikhail

Present

The sound of my shoes echoes in the empty anteroom of the Chicago Opera Theater, mixing with the faint opening notes of *Swan Lake* coming from the hallway on the left. With the ballet already starting, the entrance is vacated. I nod to the security guy, then turn and follow the long hallway toward the double wooden doors at the far end, where a poster hanging on the wall attracts my attention.

They've changed the photo. The previous one showed the whole troupe in the middle of a group jump, taken from afar so the whole stage was visible; but the new one shows only one dancer, the shot zoomed in. I take a step closer until I'm standing right before the image. Without conscious thought, my hand rises and traces the contours of her face—her sharp cheekbones, her cherry-blossom mouth, down her slender neck, then back up over the outline of her eyes, which seem to be looking straight at me. The big letters at the top of the poster announce this evening's show as her last performance. Looks like the season is closing.

Sometimes, I imagine approaching her, maybe after one of her shows. We would exchange a few words and I would invite her to dinner. Nothing fancy, perhaps that cozy tavern downtown. They have the best wine and . . . I catch my reflection visible on the glass covering the poster, and I instantly let my hand fall back, feeling like my touch somehow tainted her. I guess this is as close as someone like me—hideous inside and out—should be allowed near such perfection.

I carefully open the big wooden door and quietly slip inside. With the only source of light coming from the stage, the space is rather obscure, but I still keep myself to the back where the darkness is the thickest. I've been extremely careful in pursuing my obsession, always making sure I arrive after the show starts and leave before it ends. It's better to keep a low profile. Saying I don't blend into the crowd would be an understatement.

My looks have never really bothered me. In my line of business, the scarier you look, the easier it is to make people talk. Sometimes, the only thing needed was for me to enter the room and they would spill all they know. My reputation has helped as well.

Finding a suitable fuck was usually tricky, but it had nothing to do with my face. A lot of women from our circle were eager to lure the Bratva's Butcher into their bed, but they became significantly less eager when I presented them with the rules: only remove enough clothes to get the job done, strictly from behind, and no touching of any kind.

The civilians had different reactions. Most tended to

avoid looking directly at me. Others liked to stare. I was perfectly fine with either approach.

So, why the fuck does it bother me now? Why am I hiding in dark corners, stalking this girl I've only seen from afar, like a psycho? I'm still debating my sanity when the solo violin theme begins and my eyes snap back to the stage. I know nothing about music, but I haven't missed any of her shows for months, and by now, I recognize exactly when her entrance comes. When my gaze finds her gliding toward the center of the stage, I feel my breath catch in my chest.

She's a vision, spinning along the stage in her long gauzy skirt, and I am mesmerized as I follow each of her moves. Her light blonde hair is twisted at the back of her neck, but instead of making her look stern, the harsh hairstyle only accentuates her perfect doll-like features. She's like a little bird—gracious and fragile—and God . . . so painfully young. I lean on the wall behind me and shake my head. If I don't break out of this madness, I'll go crazy.

After her part is finished, I leave, but instead of going straight to the exit, I make a detour to the big table near the backstage door. It's packed with flower arrangements visitors have left to be sent to the dancers' dressing rooms. Strange setup, but it works for me. As always, I leave a single rose and proceed to the exit.

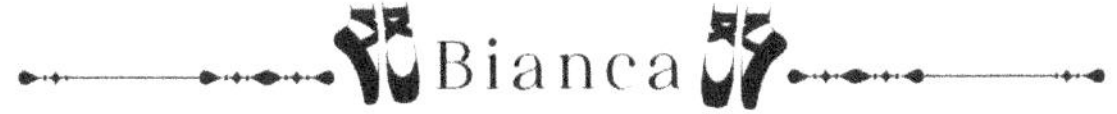

"Your father wants to talk with you," my mother says from the doorway.

I ignore her and wrap the last of my costumes in thin white paper, tracing the gauzy fabric of the tulle skirt along the way. Then, I pack it into the big white box on my bed, where I've already stored the rest of my stage outfits and secure the lid over it. Everything that remains of my career as a professional dancer, ready to collect dust. I never expected it to end so quickly. The star of the Chicago Opera Theater, who rose to the position of principal dancer in her company at sixteen. Now retired at barely twenty-one years of age. Fifteen years of hard work just gone because of one stupid injury. As I turn to place the box at the bottom of the closet, I want to weep, but I keep the tears from falling. What's the point anyway?

"He's in his office," my mother continues. "Don't make him wait, Bianca. It's important."

I wait for her to leave, then start toward the door only to stop in front of my vanity and look at the crystal vase holding a single yellow rose. Usually, I donate all the flowers I get after a performance to the children's hospital. This is the only one I keep. I reach out with my hand and trace the long thornless stem wrapped in a yellow silk ribbon with gold details. There has been one left for me after every performance for the past six months. No message. No signature. Nothing. Well, this is the last one I'll ever get.

I exit my room and head downstairs to the furthest part of the house where my father's and brother's offices are situated. The dull pain in my back is almost gone now, but I stopped deluding myself it was just a passing thing months ago. I will never be able to withstand six-hour practices, five days a week, again.

The door to my father's office is open, so I go inside without knocking, close the door behind me, and stand in front of his desk. He doesn't acknowledge me, just keeps scribbling notes in his leather organizer. Bruno Scardoni never acknowledges people he considers beneath him a second sooner than he feels fit. He enjoys seeing them fidget while he practices his might over them. Unfortunately, I never really gave a fuck about his power games, so I sit in the chair opposite him without an invitation and cross my arms over my chest.

"Ill-behaving, as ever, I see," he says without lifting his head from the organizer. "I'm glad your disobedience will soon become someone else's problem."

My heartbeat speeds up at his words, but I school my features so as not to show any reaction. Father is like a predator, just waiting for his prey to show weakness so he can attack, aiming for the jugular.

"We're signing a truce with the Russians," he says and looks up at me. "And you're getting married to one of Petrov's men next week."

It takes me a few seconds to collect myself from the shock, then I look my father right in the eyes and mouth "No."

"It wasn't a question, Bianca. Everything is already agreed upon—a daughter of a capo for one of his men. Congratulations, *cara mia*." A poisonous smile spreads across his face.

I grab a piece of paper and a pen from his desk, quickly write the words and pass it toward him. He looks down at the note and grinds his teeth.

"I can't make you?" he sneers.

I start to stand up, but he leans toward me, grabs my arm, and slaps me across my face so hard my head snaps to the side. My ears are ringing, but I take a deep breath, turn toward my father again, and slowly take the paper from where he threw it on the other side of the desk. I straighten the edges of the paper, place it on the desk in front of him, point my finger to the words written there, and head toward the door. I won't be married off, especially to some Russian brute.

"If you don't do it, I'll give them Milene."

His words stop me in my tracks. He wouldn't dare. My little sister is only eighteen. She's still a child. I turn around, look my father in the eyes, and I see it. He would.

"I see that got your attention. Good." He points to the chair I just vacated. "Get back here."

The five steps I take to that chair are probably the second hardest thing I've done in my life. My feet feel like they are made of lead the whole way back.

"Now, since that's settled, a few things. You will be a docile, dutiful wife to your husband. I still don't know who it'll be, but it doesn't matter. What's important is the fact he'll be someone from Petrov's inner circle."

I watch him as he leans back in his chair and takes a cigar from the box in front of him.

"You'll rein in your temper, let him fuck you as much as he wants, and make sure he trusts you. He'll probably underestimate you, as people usually do when they find out you can't speak, and he'll start opening up, babbling about business." He points his cigar in my direction. "You will remember everything he says, every single detail about how they are organized, what routes they use for distribution, everything he might mention."

Opening a drawer in his desk, he takes out a burner phone, and slides it across the desk toward me. "You will message me everything you learn. Every single thing. Do you understand, Bianca?"

Everything makes more sense now. What a perfect setup he's made: get rid of his problematic child, and get into good graces with the don by sacrificing one of his daughters to the Bratva, all while making sure he'll be the one getting the inside information on the Russians. Brilliant, really.

"I asked you a question!" he snarls.

I tilt my head to the side and regard him, wishing I had a gun and imagining pointing it between his eyes and pulling the trigger. I wouldn't miss. Over the years, my brother's made sure my aim is impeccable by secretly taking me with him on his shooting practices. I'm not sure I'd have the guts to kill my father but imagining it definitely feels good.

I nod, collect the phone from the desk, and leave the office, catching sight of his satisfied smile from the corner of my eye. Let him believe whatever he wants. I might be marrying into the Bratva, but I'm doing it for my sister, not because he's ordered me to. And I'm not playing his spy. I am not dying because of him, again.

Mikhail

When Roman Petrov, Bratva's *pakhan*, enters the dining room, everybody stands and stays standing until he takes a seat at the head of the table. He leans his cane on his chair and nods for us to sit back down. The first chair on his right remains empty. His wife probably feels unwell again. I thought pregnant women only had sickness in the morning, but based on what I heard in the kitchen, Nina Petrova has been vomiting nonstop for weeks.

Roman turns to the maid and motions with his head toward the door. "Leave and close the door, Valentina. I'll call you when we're done."

She nods quickly and rushes out of the room, closing the double doors behind her. It looks like we'll be discussing business before dinner. Roman leans back in his chair, and I wonder what kind of bomb he'll be dropping on us today. The last time he called us all in, he informed us he secretly got married two days after meeting his wife.

"As you already know, we're calling a truce with the Italians," he says. "They've agreed to my terms, I've agreed to theirs, and the only thing left is to organize a wedding to seal the deal." He raises his eyebrows. "So, who would like to volunteer to be the lucky groom?"

Nobody says a word. We don't do arranged marriages in the Bratva. That was always an Italian thing, and nobody wants to be saddled with a Trojan horse. That's what the woman would be, and everybody knows it. I wonder who he'll pick. It won't be me, because Roman knows my issues too well. It won't be Sergei, either. No one in their right state of mind would trust that lunatic with a toaster, let alone a human being. Maxim is too old, so I'm betting on Kostya or Ivan.

"What, no one wants a pretty Italian girl? Maybe this will help change your mind." He reaches into the pocket of his jacket, takes out a photo, and passes it to Maxim. "Bianca Scardoni, the middle daughter of Italian capo Bruno Scardoni, and up until recently, the prima ballerina of the Chicago Opera Theater."

I feel my body go stone-still. It's not possible.

"They really want this alliance." Roman smiles. "The most beautiful woman of the Italian Mafia is up for grabs."

Maxim passes the picture to Pavel, crosses his arms over his chest, and looks at Roman. "What's the catch?"

"Why do you think there would be a catch?"

"The Italians would never give up a capo's daughter, especially one who looks like that, to the Bratva. No matter how much they want an alliance. There must be something wrong with her."

"Well, there is one small catch, but I'd rather call it a bonus." Roman smirks.

I take the photo Pavel passes me and look down at it. She's even more beautiful with her loose hair framing her perfect face, while her light brown eyes are smiling into the camera. Grinding my teeth, I pass the picture to Ivan. Just thinking about one of my comrades getting her makes a wave of rage come over me, and I grab the arms of the chair with all my might, so I won't end up hitting something.

Ivan looks at the image, his eyebrows raised, then nudges Dimitri with his elbow and passes him the photo.

"She doesn't look . . . extremely Italian." Dimitri nods at the photo in his hands "I thought all Italian girls had dark hair. Was she adopted?"

"Nope. Maternal grandmother was Norwegian," Roman throws in.

Sergei is next, but he just passes the photo to Kostya, without even looking at it.

"Fuck, she's hot." Kostya whistles and shakes his head. "Do you have another photo? Preferably with fewer clothes."

Focusing on the wall across from me, I squeeze the chair even harder, trying to control the urge to get up and punch Kostya in the face or do something worse, like claim her for myself. Kostya keeps looking at the photo, and for a moment,

I imagine him placing his hands on her and my control disintegrates in a fraction of a second.

"I'll take her," I say.

The absolute silence fills the room as all eyes focus on me, surprise and disbelief visible on every face. I turn to Roman who regards me with his eyebrows raised.

"An interesting development," he says. "I was planning to give her to Kostya if no one volunteered. He's closest to her age."

"Well, he's not getting her."

"You still haven't heard the catch, Mikhail. You may change your mind."

"I won't change my mind."

"Well." Roman shrugs and takes a sip of his drink. "That's settled then."

The dinner passes in silence, which is unusual. Instead of business talk and a laugh here and there, tonight, everyone seems preoccupied with their meal, but I notice the guys throwing looks in my direction from time to time. They're probably wondering what's gotten into me to claim the Italian girl for myself, but I don't care what they think. She's mine, no matter what.

After the meal is over, Roman gives me a nod, and I follow him down the long corridor into his office. He sits down on the recliner in the corner while I remain standing and lean on the wall behind me.

"She's twenty-one. You are too old for her, Mikhail."

"Ten years is not much. You're eleven years older than your wife."

"I have an extremely youthful personality," he says and smiles.

"Sure."

"Eloquent as ever." He shakes his head. "She's barely an adult. What will you do when she starts pestering you about going out every night? What if she wants to go partying, and you have to tell her you need to work? You'll have to take her to watch teen movies every week. Even Nina loves that crap. I can ask her to send you some recommendations, you know."

"Thank you. I'll pass."

Roman sighs and leans back. "Girls her age want a man who'll speak more than five sentences a day, Mikhail. They expect kisses, cuddling. Did you think about that?"

"We'll work it out."

Silence. He's just watching me with his head tilted to the side, and I know exactly what he's pondering.

"She's not one of your regular fucks. How do you expect a twenty-one-year-old girl to deal with your . . . issues?"

"She won't have to. I'll deal with my issues myself."

"Oh? When was the last time you voluntarily touched someone other than Lena?"

I stare at him without answering. Not because I don't want to, but because I can't remember. "I'll deal with it, Roman."

"Are you sure?"

"Yes."

"All right then." He sighs and continues, "You know she will likely be spying on us and reporting to the Italians. You're in charge of most of our drug operations, so I need you to be very careful about what you say in front of her. Also, make sure you remove all sensitive information from your office in case she decides to snoop around when you're not there."

"I will."

"There's one more thing you need to know about her, and if you decide to change your mind, I'll saddle Kostya with her."

"I won't change my mind."

"She doesn't speak, Mikhail."

I stiffen and look at Roman, not sure if I heard him right.

"She can't be deaf," I say. "She's a dancer."

"She isn't deaf. There was a car accident when she was a teenager. I don't have any details. It's all Scardoni shared."

"How does she communicate?"

"I have no idea. Writes in a notebook or sign language, I suppose. Are you still in?"

"Yes."

Roman raises an eyebrow but doesn't comment on my decision. "Do you want me to set up a meeting before we do the wedding?"

I feel myself go still. "No."

"Why?" he asks, as if he doesn't already know the answer to that question. "She can't say no. Everything is already settled."

"No meeting."

Roman watches me, then shakes his head. "Let's organize the wedding then."

Chapter Two

Bianca

MORNING SUNLIGHT ENTERS THE ROOM through gauzy drapes on the windows, bathing it in warmth. It would make such a perfect day for a wedding, if it wasn't mine. It might be warm outside, but inside of me, an ice storm is raging.

I lean forward, place the tip of the eyeliner at the corner of my eye, and pull a long thin line on my eyelid. Maybe I should have run away. They would have found me eventually, but it would've been worth it.

"You're so beautiful!" Milene exclaims from the doorway and rushes into my room. "I'm going to cry!"

I smile for my sister's sake and continue applying makeup. For someone who hates weddings, she's been unusually excited about the whole thing, so I couldn't make myself tell her the truth.

"I wish Angelo was here to see you, he was so mad when Dad made him go to Mexico."

Yeah, I wish my brother was here today, too. He's the only

family member, other than Milene, who actually cares about me, and I'm pretty certain Father sent him away on purpose.

"I made Agosto take me to see the reception hall at six this morning. It's amazing. I still can't believe you agreed to an arranged marriage. I always thought we'd stay spinsters together, living alone with a bunch of cats."

She starts fumbling with my dress, soothing the material. "I'm totally living vicariously through you today. It's the closest I plan on getting to a wedding. Ever." Laughing, she bends to check the hem of the dress while I watch her in the mirror.

Milene has no idea how close she came to being in my place today. She plans on going to college after high school. Becoming a nurse is all she's talked about since she turned eight, and it's all she's ever wanted. I hope her wish comes true. Knowing how stubborn Milene is, she'll probably make it, unless our father decides to also marry her off before she escapes his clutches.

"So, tell me about him. I want to know everything about your future husband! Why didn't you bring him to meet us?"

I leave the eyeliner on the vanity and turn on my chair to face Milene, my sweet baby sister who spent hours of her free time on YouTube and learned sign language because of me. My mother and brother learned the basics as well, but they only practiced enough to understand simple sentences. My older sister, Allegra, and my father never bothered.

"*His name is Mikhail Orlov,*" I sign. Milene has gotten so much better in sign language over the last few years, that we can have a normal conversation, but she still needs me to go slow.

"And? What does he look like? Is he hot? How old is he? Come on, tell me."

"That's all I know."

"Oh, don't be so secretive." Milene laughs and pinches my upper arm. "Tell me!"

"We have never met. And I don't know anything else except his name." The truth is, I don't care, so I never asked. What good would it do me? I'm marrying the man whether I want it or not.

"What! Are you crazy? I though you at least met him and decided to go through with this marriage because you liked the guy."

"Go change. We'll be late."

"Bianca?" She places her hand on my shoulder. "Did you agree to the marriage? Or is Father making you do this?"

"Of course, I did."

"You agreed to marry someone you never met? Don't lie to me, love."

"I'm not lying. Please go change."

She regards me through narrowed eyes, but eventually leaves. I finish my makeup, put on my heels, and head into my unhappily ever after, praying that Milene won't face the same fate.

Mikhail

The wedding is set to take place in the reception hall of the luxury Four Seasons hotel in the center of Chicago, and as soon as we arrive, all heads turn toward us. Dozens of gazes follow our path as Roman and the rest of the group sit in the first two rows on the right side. There are only eight of us in total, whereas the left side, where the Italians are sitting, is packed full. All twenty rows are occupied with grim faces. I guess no one is happy with one of their own marrying into the Bratva, but that certainly didn't deter them from coming for gossip and free food.

Italians seriously invest themselves into their celebrations and appearances. There are huge, white, flower arrangements everywhere and silk ribbons tied into bows around each chair. They even put a bunch of white petals all over the damn floor. For Italians, it's always about making a great impression.

While the others sit down, Kostya and I stand near the first row. The Italians start talking among themselves, nudging each other with their elbows, watching us. Most of them move their eyes away the moment they see my face and focus on Kostya, sizing him up. With his longish blond hair and mischievous smile, Kostya is a pretty kid. Women have always thrown themselves at him, so it's not surprising that these people have concluded he's the one getting married today.

I take a step forward and stand at the front, where the wedding officiant waits on the other side of the high table. Kostya, my best man, follows but stops two steps to my right. The moment it becomes evident that I'm the groom, there is a collective gasp, and the whole room goes silent.

I face the crowd of Italians, who stare at me with shock evident in their eyes and pass over them with my gaze until I reach Bruno Scardoni. Isn't he supposed to escort his daughter down the aisle? He's sitting in the middle of the first row, a smug, self-satisfied smile on his lips. Interesting. The three women on his right, his wife and two daughters, are sitting stone-still, a look of horror on their faces. That, at least, is expected. I wonder where the brother is. From the information

I've gathered, Bianca and her brother are close, so it's strange for him to miss his sister's wedding.

Just as I start wondering if I should've had that meeting with Bianca before the wedding, the sounds of the wedding march fill the room. I hope she won't run off screaming upon seeing me, because I will be chasing.

Bianca

I regard the white door in front of me and wonder what kind of life waits for me on the other side. Catalina, my cousin and bridesmaid today, fidgets with the veil, arranging the folds to fall over my face.

Sold. I'm being sold like cattle to ensure someone else's goals bear fruit. There was nothing I could have done to avoid this, other than ruin my sister's life in exchange for my own. I can't go back, so I'll go forward with my head held high and my asshole father see he hasn't broken me.

He threw such a fit when I told him I would be walking down the aisle by myself. "What would people say?" he yelled.

What people say makes no difference to me. I have no intention of having the man who decided to use me as collateral damage play a dutiful father. And I certainly won't go in there with my face covered like I'm some demure scared victim.

A man in a hotel uniform opens the door when the first notes of the wedding march starts play. I grab the hem of the veil, remove the damn thing from my head, and drop the lacy fabric on the floor. Catalina gasps behind me, but I ignore her and take a deep breath, and step into the reception hall.

Mikhail

The woman I've been obsessing about for months steps inside the room, and I feel my breath leave my lungs. I knew she was beautiful, but seeing her this close and in person . . . I was so wrong. She's not just beautiful, that word is too plain. Wearing the long white dress that flows over her body and ends in a short train, she is breathtaking. Soft blonde curls are falling freely on either side of her face and down to her waist. I don't think I've ever seen a woman with hair that long. She reminds me of an elven princess. I wonder what kind of monster I would be in that story.

Her head held high, she walks down the aisle with sure, quick steps, right toward me. She looks at me and holds my gaze, not a flinch upon seeing my ruined face and the eyepatch, not a falter in her step while she approaches. I expected a shy, timid girl, scared of the situation she's been thrown into, but there's no trace of fear in those eyes, just determination.

She stands before me, so beautiful and defiant, and I have this sudden, unexplainable need to touch her. To make sure she is real. It's a strange feeling. I don't enjoy skin contact with anyone except Lena. I don't like it and I never initiate it.

The wedding officiant starts speaking, and as we turn toward him, I can't resist brushing my finger over the back of her hand. It's a small touch. I'm sure she won't even notice it. The man in front of us keeps babbling, and I look down to steal another glance at my bride. She's on the short side and her tiny hand looks so delicate next to mine. Breakable. But then she looks up, and there is nothing fragile in those eyes that regard me without blinking.

Bianca

He is not what I expected.

As the wedding officiant starts reciting his part, I don't hear a word of what he says. My whole being is focused on the man standing by my side. When I entered the room and my eyes landed on his huge frame at the end of the aisle, I almost stumbled, and only the years of practice I had on the stage made me keep moving forward. My future husband is built like a professional fighter, his wide shoulders straining the material of his jacket. He's wearing a black shirt and black dress pants, and with his ink-black hair and that eyepatch, he looks like a dark avenging angel.

I didn't notice the scars right away because I was too focused on his imposing figure. The largest scar starts above his right eyebrow and runs straight down his face, disappearing under the eyepatch and then continuing down to his jaw. There is another one next to it, starting from somewhere under the eyepatch and trailing down to a point slightly above the corner of his lips. The one on the left side of his chin, runs the length of his neck and disappears under the collar of his dress shirt. I have no idea what could have happened to him to inflict such wounds, but it must have been something horrific. Most men I know would have grown a beard to conceal at least some of the lines marring their face. Looks like my soon-to-be husband doesn't hide his scars, because he is clean-shaven, as if he doesn't give a fuck what other people might think.

The wedding officiant finishes his speech, and the man standing next to my groom approaches and places a small velvet box containing the wedding rings on the table. Mikhail takes the smaller one and looks at me, waiting. I raise my hand and watch as he slides the ring onto my finger without touching my skin. It seems like he's deliberately avoided doing so. I take the big wedding ring from the box and raise it, but instead of offering his hand, he takes the ring from between my fingers and slides it onto his finger himself.

The officiant pronounces us husband and wife, and motions toward the big open book lying on the table. There was no "you may kiss the bride" part, and I wonder if that was intentional or if he forgot, because the man seems strangely distressed, fidgeting with his hands, looking anywhere except at my husband.

Mikhail takes the pen, writes his name, and offers it to me. I look up and find him watching me like he's expecting me to turn and bolt. Without breaking our locked gaze, I curve an eyebrow, then take the pen from his hand and sign my name. Bianca Orlov. It's done.

Mikhail

I watch the crowd of people "attacking" the buffet tables, piling their plates with food and chatting loudly. Bianca is standing next to me, silently observing the room, and I have a feeling she's not a fan of crowds. We have that in common.

Roman approaches me, saying he's leaving with Dimitri. He's probably anxious to get back to his wife who stayed at home. I'm surprised he came to the wedding at all, considering how reluctant he is to let her leave his sight. He turns toward Bianca and introduces himself, offering his hand. When their palms connect, I'm consumed by a strange need to bat Roman's hand away, preventing him from touching my wife.

"Do you want to leave?" I ask when Roman's out of sight.

Bianca looks over the crowd, raises her head to look at me, and nods. I start toward the exit, motioning with my head to Kostya and the rest of our men. We're almost to the door when I feel Bianca's hand touch my forearm, squeezing it lightly, and I tense for a split-second before willing my muscles to relax. She glances over at the table where her family is sitting as if she wants to say goodbye, so I turn and start walking in their direction.

The younger sister jumps up from the chair and rushes toward Bianca, embracing her around the waist and whispering something in her ear. Bianca takes a step back and starts signing with her hands. Making sure nothing on my face shows recognition, I discretely watch her fingers form the words.

"We're going. Everything is okay. I'll message you in the morning and we'll talk."

"Dad will be mad if you leave so early," her sister whispers.

"You can tell Father dearest to go to hell." Bianca signs this slowly, like she wants to make sure her sister catches every word, then grabs her by the hand and turns the girl to me.

The poor thing gulps, but quickly collects herself and smiles. She doesn't offer her hand, and I'm glad for that. When necessary, I have no problem with standard social interactions, like handshakes, but prefer to avoid them.

"I'm Milene. Nice to meet you, Mr. Orlov."

It doesn't escape my attention that Milene is the only one from her family who Bianca introduces personally. With the others, I only exchange curt nods, which isn't that strange considering we were trying to kill each other not a month before.

Milene turns to say something to Bianca when a gunshot explodes through the room.

Bianca

Barely a second after the sound of the first gunshot pierces the air, a strong arm grabs me around the waist. The next thing I know, I'm plastered to the floor next to Milene, with Mikhail bent over us, protecting us from the line of fire with his body.

"The service door. Stay low. Now!" he barks over the noise of more gunshots and people screaming.

I manage to untangle my legs from the train of the dress, scoop up the fabric in one hand, and crab crawl as fast as I can behind Milene toward the door a few yards away. As soon as I make it into the narrow hallway, I lean back against the wall and grab Milene in a tight embrace. She's shaking like a leaf, her breathing labored, and I am not far behind. I throw a look toward the door, expecting to find Mikhail there, but he's not in the hallway with us.

There are two more quick bangs before the gunfire stops altogether, and the only thing I can hear are men yelling and women screaming. I wait a couple of seconds then go back toward the door and glimpse into the room. It's chaos.

People are stampeding toward the double doors on the

other side of the room, not paying attention to others around them. An older man, who I recognize as one of my father's cousins, is lying in a puddle of blood, unmoving. Not far from him, a woman is sitting on the floor with two men kneeling on either side of her, one clutching her bleeding arm. More people around the room look hurt, either by the bullets or the stampede, but no one else looks dead or seriously wounded. Several men are walking around the room with their guns drawn, checking on the wounded. I recognize a few of them as the ones who were with Mikhail, but the rest are my father's men.

Off to the side, near a wall, Mikhail is standing with a group gathered above the body of a waiter lying prone on the floor. I watch as Mikhail puts his gun in the holster hidden under his jacket and crouches next to the body. He unbuttons the dead man's right sleeve and pulls it up, inspecting his forearm. My father goes to stand next to Mikhail. They discuss something for a few seconds, then Mikhail turns and walks toward me.

"Go to your father, Milene," he says to my sister, then turns to me. "This way."

He leads me down the long hallway and through the hotel's laundry room, where the uniformed staff peek out from behind big service washing machines. We exit through a metal door and turn right toward the parking lot. It feels like I'm moving through a vacuum, not hearing anything and just barely aware of our surroundings. This is the first time I've witnessed gunfire outside of the shooting range, and I might be in shock.

Mikhail approaches a car and opens the passenger door for me. If someone asks me about the model, or even the color of the car I get into, I wouldn't be able to tell them anything. He calls someone during the drive, but the whole conversation is in Russian, so I have no idea what he says or with whom he speaks.

Shortly after he ends the call, he parks in the underground garage of a tall modern building. I haven't been paying attention to where we were going, so the only thing I know is that we're somewhere downtown.

Mikhail opens the car door for me, and I follow him to the silver elevator and watch as he passes a keycard over the small display, then presses the button for the top floor. A short time later, the elevator doors open onto a small foyer with only one door directly ahead.

I take a deep breath. He brought me to his home. I don't know why this fact hits me so hard. Of course, he would take me to his place. It wasn't like I expected him to drop me off at my father's house, but still, it's like I'm just now grasping the extent of how different my life will be from this point forward. I take another breath and enter Mikhail's home.

"Living room, dining room, kitchen, guest bathroom." Mikhail points around the huge open space lined with floor-to-ceiling windows on the opposite side. "The room I use as a gym. Lena's room. My office."

Who's Lena? Maybe he has a live-in housekeeper.

Mikhail turns and points to the other side of the open space. "My bedroom. You can have the guest room next to it."

I stare at him, processing what he just said. He won't make me sleep with him?

He looks down at me, his one blue eye regarding me with interest, and reaches with his hand to remove a strand of hair that's fallen over my face, hooking it behind my ear.

"I don't force women, Bianca. Is that clear?"

I nod.

"Good. I have to go now, and I probably won't be back before morning. There's food in the fridge. Eat. Take a shower and go to sleep, you need the rest. Give me your phone."

Somehow, the small clutch purse hanging across my chest on a thin gold chain survived this evening's events. I reach inside, take out my phone, and give it to him reluctantly. I didn't expect him to confiscate it.

Instead of taking my phone away, he starts typing.

"I'm entering my number, as well as the number of the security desk downstairs. If you need anything, you can message me. I may not be able to message you back right away, but I'll do it as soon as I can." He offers my phone back, and I slowly raise my hand and take it.

"Feel free to go around and explore, but my office is off-limits. Everything else is okay. Are we clear on that?"

I nod again and keep staring at him, expecting him to say something like "See you in the morning" or "Good night," but instead, he just reaches over and traces his finger down the back of my hand, his touch featherlight. It lasts just for a second, and then he's gone without a word.

What a strange man.

"He had an Albanian gang tattoo on the inside of his forearm," I tell Roman. "Do you think it's Dushku?"

"Possible. Maybe he found out it was me who offed his

friend Tanush. Or maybe he was mad because we beat him in making a deal with the Italians."

"It could be both." I nod. "Or someone wants us to think it was Dushku. They sent only one man, and half of the people in that room were armed. It was a suicide mission. And how very convenient that he had a tattoo connecting him to the Albanians. Something doesn't add up."

Roman leans forward, drumming his fingers on the desk. "It could be the Italians playing us, setting the stage for something bigger. They were in charge of security for the wedding, and an armed man managed to get through." He points his finger at me. "You need to watch your wife. Watch her very closely."

"I will." I nod and leave the pakhan's office.

On my way back home, I think about what Roman said. Is he right? Could Bianca be acting as a spy for her father? It would be a great opportunity—one I was sure a capo as ruthless as Bruno Scardoni wouldn't miss. Still, I have a feeling that isn't the case here. The distaste I saw in Bianca's eyes every time she looked at her father couldn't be faked. Yes, my wife has very expressive eyes.

I wonder if I should tell her I'm proficient in sign language. It would make the communication much easier, but it would lead to things I'm not ready to discuss with her yet. We'll have to manage without sign language for now.

Bianca

When I'm stressed, I either clean or cook. There is nothing here to clean. Everything is spotless. So, I head into the kitchen and start looking for ingredients to make my quick cheese pasta.

Earlier, I showered in the guest bathroom and spent some time walking around Mikhail's place. The apartment is crazy huge—spanning the whole top floor of the building and decorated in a modern style, mostly glass and dark wood combined with white accents. I checked out the kitchen first, which is a chef's dream and fully stocked. I stumbled on a few interesting items such as cocoa in the pantry, small packs of strawberry yogurt in the fridge, and a drawer full of sweets. My husband doesn't strike me as a person who likes sweets and strawberry yogurt, but hey, people have strange tastes.

Next was Mikhail's bedroom. It felt wrong poking around in there, so I just went to his closet and took the first T-shirt I saw. I was not sleeping in a towel or naked. Wearing no panties was bad enough already.

After Mikhail's bedroom, I skipped the housekeeper's room and stopped in the doorway to the gym, confused. I expected a bunch of high-end bodybuilding machines, a treadmill, and similar items. Instead, there was just a rack with old school weights of different sizes in one corner, a pull-up bar next to it, and a punching bag. Everything was lined along the wall across from the floor-to-ceiling windows, and it didn't take up even a fifth of the room. What a waste of space. He could've easily added another room in there. From the gym I went back straight to the kitchen, ignoring the door to his office.

When I finish cooking the pasta, I make myself a plate and leave the pot with the rest on the counter. I look around, searching for something to write with and some paper, and eventually find a pen in one of the drawers. No paper though.

I take the empty pasta box, tear one side, then sit at the dining table and start writing on the cardboard.

When I'm done, I leave the note on the floor next to the front door, where Mikhail can't miss it, and go back into the guest room.

Mikhail

I pick up the piece of cardboard lying on the floor and start reading.

I made pasta. I left it on the counter.

I borrowed one of your T-shirts. I hope you don't mind.

With everything that's happened, I forgot I need to drop by my father's house and pick up a bag with my clothes. Can you drop me by tomorrow to get it?

We may need to stop by a store where I can buy a change of clothes. I can't go to my father's house wearing only your T-shirt.

I couldn't find coffee in the kitchen. My name is Bianca, and I am a caffeine addict. If you have it somewhere, please message me the location before you go to sleep. I'm not the most pleasant person in the morning before I get my hit.

My lips curl slightly at that last line, and I head toward the door to the guest room, which is slightly ajar. Bundled under a thick duvet, Bianca is sleeping soundly, her hair tangled around her head. I lean onto the doorway and watch her sleeping form until the light of dawn starts seeping into the room.

Chapter Three

Bianca

It's almost nine when I wake up, and I find it rather surprising that I slept like a log for eight hours in a stranger's home. When I went to bed the previous night, I was out the moment my head hit the pillow. Maybe it's some bizarre aftereffect of being shot at.

After dropping by the bathroom to take care of my screaming bladder, and to brush my teeth, I head to the kitchen. On the counter next to the coffee machine, I find my note, one corner of it sitting under a bag of unopened coffee beans. Next to each of my notes, there are comments in neat handwriting.

Thank you.

I don't mind.

Yes.

I called my housekeeper and told her to buy something for you to wear tomorrow until we get your things. She'll leave it on the counter.

Far right cupboard, top shelf. But you can put it wherever you want.

Next to the note, there's a paper bag. I look inside and take out a pair of gray yoga pants and two T-shirts. At the bottom, there's some underwear and socks. There are no shoes, so it looks like I'll be pairing my strappy heels with yoga pants and a T-shirt when we go to get my things. Classy.

After a small detour to the guest room to put on some underwear, I make myself a cup of coffee, grab a banana from the bowl, and climb onto a tall chair at the breakfast bar separating the kitchen and the dining room. I should probably message Milene.

> **09:22 Bianca:** Just checking in to let you know that everything is okay. Did Uncle Fredo survive? Was anyone else seriously hurt yesterday? Are you okay?
>
> **09:23 Milene:** He's gone. I heard Dad this morning saying Fredo was only spending the family's money and I quote, "At least something good came out of that wedding." Agapito's lover got a bullet in her arm, but I think that's it. Can't wait to leave this idiotic life.
>
> **09:26 Bianca:** Father won't finance your college, Milene.
>
> **09:28 Milene:** Nonna Giulia said she'll pay for it. Three more months and bye bye Cosa Nostra bullshit. Dad is going to lose it, ha ha! Is everything okay there? I want the full report. How did it go? How is he? Did you have to sleep with him?

09:25 Bianca: He's okay, I guess. A little strange. Doesn't talk much. He just dropped me off yesterday and went somewhere. Work, I think. I haven't seen him since.

09:26 Milene: WTF? On his wedding night? I guess you were lucky. I have to go, the teacher is coming over.

There are two more new messages, one from my mother and one from Angelo. I read Angelo's text first.

02:11 Angelo: Congratulations sis. Who's the lucky groom? The connection here is awful, I didn't hear half of the things Dad said when he called.

I look at the message and sigh. Angelo never found anything wrong with the tradition of arranged marriages. It was expected, and, therefore, must be done. From what I've overheard, Father already arranged for him to marry Don Agostini's granddaughter. But Isabella and Angelo already know each other. It's not the same situation, though, and I'd be lying if I said I expected him to be so blasé.

09:29 Bianca: Mikhail Orlov. When are you coming back? And what are you doing in Mexico anyway?

The next message is from Mom. I open it and a bunch of text fills the screen. I groan, decrease the font size, and start reading her essay.

07:44 Mom: You were so beautiful yesterday. Everybody talked about it. And that dress was worth every penny. Catalina's mother asked me

> where we purchased it so she can order one for Catalina. That woman is always copying us. I can't stand her. Too bad everything ended so abruptly. I can't believe Fredo got shot and died, but I guess it's better him than someone else. He was over eighty. Did you notice that Luca Rossi came alone? Simona never liked me, but to miss your wedding? I never understood how those two ended up together. It's such a shame for a man like Luca to end up with a bitch like her. Someone should tell him it's time for him to cut that hair of his, it's not proper. He's a capo, for God's sake.

I close my eyes and sigh. My mom's priorities have always been rather strange. It's not her fault. If she wasn't a capo's wife, I'm positive she would have been a serial killer, or something similar. It's not like she was diagnosed, but I'm almost certain my mother is a borderline sociopath. I wonder at which point in her message she'll ask about how I'm handling being married to a stranger. I continue reading her novel-length text.

> Since you're done with ballet, you'll have more free time now. We should go shopping together one day, I'm sure the distraction would do you good. I have no idea what your father was thinking when he agreed to marry you to that man. Honestly, I'm glad I didn't have my glasses yesterday, so I couldn't see that well. I tried contacts again yesterday morning, but my eyes started itching. Maybe I should try another brand. Allegra says he's monstrous. Is that true? You should have married Marcus . . .

I take a sip of my coffee. Allegra . . . always putting her nose where it doesn't belong. No, it's not true. The man has one eye, so what? It's not like he's missing half his brain, like Marcus. As for his character . . . I can't say. We didn't interact much, so I can't conclude what kind of man he is. But when that first shot rang out, he covered me and my sister with his body. And that says a lot. Reluctantly, I finish reading.

> How is he treating you? If he raises his voice at you, just let me know and I'll have your father talk to him. No one treats capo's daughter with anything less than respect. Please use protection, you're too young for kids. Love you.

Yeah, like my father respects me.

> **09:42 Bianca:** Everything is okay. I'll let you know about shopping.

I put my phone down and reach for the coffee cup when the door to the gym opens and Mikhail comes out. It takes tremendous control to keep my jaw from dropping to the floor. Yesterday he was wearing a suit, but even with his jacket on, I noticed he's packing a nice muscle mass underneath. Now, he's wearing sweats and a long-sleeved T-shirt which stretches over his impossibly wide shoulders and muscled arms. The man is a powerhouse.

"I'm going to shower and then we can go get your things," he says and walks toward his bedroom.

I follow him with my eyes, feeling a little like a creep. There were a lot of guys in the dance company, and they were all extremely fit, but none of them looked like Mikhail does. I've never met anyone who looked like that. He could probably bench press me for hours without even breaking a sweat.

When I emerge from my room thirty minutes later, wearing my killer outfit of a T-shirt, yoga pants, and strappy heels with sequins, Mikhail is waiting for me by the door. I expected him to be in a suit again, but it looks like he's not working today since he's wearing faded black jeans and a black Henley shirt. The man genuinely likes black and, apparently, long sleeves.

In the garage, Mikhail leads me toward a monstrous SUV. I'm pretty sure it's not the same car we arrived in last night, because I have no idea how I'm going to get into that thing in my heels. The floor is at least two and a half feet high off the ground.

Mikhail opens the door for me, and I reach out to take ahold of something to help me up when his hands grasp me around the waist.

"Need a lift?" he asks in a completely serious tone, his face just a few inches from mine.

He doesn't wait for my reply, just lifts me up, deposits me onto the seat, and closes the door.

"Did you find everything you needed last night?" he asks after he gets in the vehicle. "I told the housekeeper to buy you some basics."

I nod. There was a big basket with bodywash, shampoo, conditioner, a toothbrush, toothpaste, and even a new hairbrush left in the bathroom.

"If you need anything else, message me the list and I'll send someone to buy it."

He starts the car while I pretend to look at the sidewalk, but secretly, I watch him from the corner of my eye. Does he find this situation strange as well? Did he choose to get married, or did his boss order him to? What if he has a girlfriend?

Will he continue seeing her? What if he brings her to his apartment while I'm there? Does he expect me to sleep with him?

I let my gaze travel up his arm, noting the contours of hard muscles visible even under his sleeve. He seems focused on the road, and since I'm sitting on his blind side and leaning back in my seat, I'm pretty sure he doesn't notice me watching him. I take the opportunity to inspect his face better. Whatever happened to him, it's not recent. Those scars look old. The interesting thing is, I don't mind them at all. Actually, I find my husband extremely handsome, so physically, I have no complaints whatsoever.

The car slows down and stops at a red light. Mikhail turns his head toward me and pins me with his gaze. I guess I'm busted, but I don't look away. He doesn't say anything, doesn't call me out for my staring, just watches me until the light changes to green. Then, he turns back to the road and keeps driving. I don't think I've ever met such a composed, controlled person. His face is completely expressionless. I can't deduce anything from it. Is he angry because I was staring at him? Or maybe he doesn't give a damn. Strange, strange man.

Mikhail parks the car in front of my father's house and comes around just as I'm opening my door. He places his hands on my waist again and helps me down. The moment my feet reach the ground, he quickly removes his hands.

"Take only what you need for the next two days. I'll send someone for the rest. It will be best if I wait for you here."

"Five minutes," I mouth the words, turn and rush inside

the house, hoping I won't meet anyone on the way to my room. Milene is at school, and there is no one else I care to see.

"Dear God, Bianca." Allegra's voice reaches me from behind as I'm heading upstairs. "How can you bear being near that monster?"

I stop at the bottom of the stairs and turn to face my older sister, who's standing with her hands on her hips, looking at me with distaste. For some reason, Allegra's always hated my guts and does her best to put me down with her poisonous comments. She even did so when we were kids. Angelo once said she was jealous of me, which is ridiculous because Allegra has always been the perfect daughter. Everyone always adores her, while I'm seen as a black sheep in our family, a pretty but flawed girl who couldn't speak.

I take two steps in her direction and stop right in front of her. Reaching out to grasp for her hand, I look at her bare ring finger, mocking sadness, then pat the back of her hand and lift my own bearing the wedding ring. Having made my point, I flip her off and leave her staring daggers at my back. I know my sister's weak points well, and I don't have a problem exploiting them. Allegra's main goal in life has always been to get married. She started making plans for her wedding day in the fourth grade. In her narrow-minded brain, my getting married before her was the most disastrous thing that could have happened.

My actions are petty, I know, but I couldn't control myself. No one gets to speak like that about my husband. We may have an arranged marriage, but he's treated me better in the last twenty-four hours than some of my family members ever have. And I'll be damned if I'll allow my sister to say something like that without hitting back.

In my room, I grab the bag I'd previously packed and turn to leave, only to find my father blocking the doorway.

"I expected a report last night, Bianca."

I step forward, intending to pass by him, but he squeezes my forearm and pushes his face up against mine.

"Where's the phone I gave you?"

Making sure that every ounce of disgust I feel for him is visible on my face, I look up and point at the trash can next to the door, where I disposed of the phone the same day he gave it to me. He looks down at it, grinds his teeth, and slaps me across my cheek. A solid open-palmed blow has always been his favorite way of showing his displeasure with me.

"You will regret your disobedience, girl," he sneers in my face and leaves.

I put the bag down and rush to the bathroom to splash some cold water on my face, and check for damage in the mirror. No broken lip this time, but there's a huge red mark covering most of my left cheek. Shit. I splash a bit more water onto it, then collect my bag on the way out of my room and leave the house in a hurry.

Mikhail is waiting for me outside, leaning casually with his back against the hood, but the moment he sees the mark on my face, he straightens and stares intently into my eyes. I bow my head and keep walking, a wave of shame engulfing me. I know I shouldn't be ashamed—it's not my fault I have an asshole for a parent—but I still am.

Mikhail's hand enters my field of vision as he places a finger under my chin and tilts my head up. He turns my head slightly to the side, inspecting my cheek.

"Your father?" he asks through clenched teeth, and I nod. "You know, I changed my mind." He takes my bag and throws it onto the passenger seat through the window. "I would love to have a word with my father-in-law."

"No," I mouth and shake my head.

"I'm going to talk with Bruno," he says in a calm voice. "You can stay here, or you can come in with me. There is a much better chance he'll get out of that conversation alive if you come."

I take a deep breath and lead him into the house.

Mikhail enters my father's office without knocking, leisurely walks to his desk, and sits down in the chair I've frequented quite often. I close the door and lean on it, not interested in getting any closer to my father than absolutely necessary.

"How dare you come in here unannounced?" my father barks. "Get out of my house!"

"It looks like I've missed spelling out some ground rules for you, Bruno."

"Rules? Are you serious?" My father laughs, stands up, and hits the table in front of him with his palm. "Who the fuck do you think you are?"

It happens so quickly I barely manage to follow. Mikhail takes the decorative letter opener with one hand and my father's wrist with the other and plunges the thing right through the center of dear old Daddy's palm and into the wooden desk.

The cry of pain that leaves my father's mouth is chilling and would have brought everyone inside the house rushing to his office if it wasn't soundproofed. He was always paranoid about someone overhearing his secret conversations.

"Shut up, Bruno," Mikhail says and leans back in his chair. "And don't even think about pressing the alarm button I know you have under the desk. I'll snap your neck before anyone arrives to save you."

Miraculously, my father stops yelling, and the only remaining sounds are his labored breaths. He grabs the handle of the letter opener and tries to pull it out, but it doesn't budge.

"Now, let's clear up a few things," Mikhail says. "You touch my wife again, in any way, I cut off your hand. I hear you speak badly about her, I cut out your tongue. You dare to even think about hitting her ever again, I cut off your head. Am I clear, Bruno?"

Instead of answering, my father just stares, his eyes wide like a madman's.

"I don't think you heard me, Bruno. How about now?" Mikhail takes the handle of the letter opener that's still embedded in my father's hand and starts rotating it.

"Yes!"

"Perfect." Mikhail stands up and heads toward me. "Have a nice day, Bruno."

I throw a look at my father, who's staring at Mikhail's back, smile, and follow my husband out of the room.

I park the car, turn off the ignition, and look at Bianca. "Why did he hit you?"

It's taken me close to an hour to calm down enough to be able to speak about it. If I asked her while we were still close to her father's house, I probably would have turned the car around and returned to kill the son of a bitch.

Bianca is staring ahead, her eyes are glassy as if she's debating with herself on whether to answer me or not. After a moment, she takes her phone, types a few words, and turns the display toward me.

He wanted me to spy on the Bratva for him. I declined.

Well, it's nothing I wasn't already expecting. "Why did you decline?"

She raises one eyebrow, types again, and gives me the phone.

I am not suicidal.

"Wise decision."

I reach out and trace my finger down her cheek, keeping the touch light. Her skin is so soft and touching it doesn't bother me. Just the opposite. I brush her cheek once more, with the back of my hand this time. The redness has vanished almost completely. I should have killed that son of a bitch anyway.

The look on Mikhail's face as he caresses my cheek is extremely puzzling. I can't describe it. Maybe somewhere between surprise and confusion, but I might be wrong because neither of those make sense. He notices me watching him and removes his hand. I wish he hadn't.

"Come on. Sisi's probably prepared something for us to eat."

Sisi? I thought the housekeeper's name was Lena.

We go to the elevator and ride up in silence. I wonder if the quietness is normal for him, or if he simply doesn't feel the need to talk since I can't reply. He opens the apartment door for me, and I go inside and stop in my tracks.

Five yards from the door, and looking right at me, stands a little girl in a pretty pink dress, her dark hair gathered in pigtails at the top of her head. She can't be more than three or maybe four, and she's the spitting image of Mikhail.

"Hello," she says, her face serious, and cocks her head to the side as she regards me with interest.

"Lenochka . . ." Mikhail says from behind me and steps inside.

"Daddy!" The girl squeals in delight, her lips widening in a huge grin as she runs and jumps into Mikhail's arms.

I watch in awe while he gathers her up and places a kiss on her cheek and then on her forehead, his hand caressing the back of her head the whole time. Mikhail has a child. I'm still processing that fact when she leans in and kisses him on the eyepatch, giggling, and Mikhail smiles.

I can't stop staring, amazed at the transformation I'm witnessing. It seems like a completely different person took his place. And it's not just the smile. The posture of his body is different, relaxed. The way he's looking at her with such warmth . . . this man has nothing in common with the cold, controlled one I married yesterday.

Still holding the girl on his hip, Mikhail turns toward me, and our gazes connect.

"This is my daughter, Lena."

So many questions run though my head. Why hasn't he said anything before? Is she living with him? Where's her mother? Does she know who I am? What if she doesn't like me? Instead of asking anything, I smile and wave.

"Lenochka, this is Bianca. You remember what we talked about?"

"Yes. Bianca is going to live with us," the girl says in her small voice, then looks over at me. "You're so pretty. Want to play? I have new toys. Daddy, Daddy, can I show Bianca my toys?"

She says all that in one breath, and I can't help but laugh at how cute she is. I want to reach out and touch her little hand, but it doesn't seem appropriate. And I don't want to scare her since we've just met. I hope she'll like me. I love kids.

"Later, zayka. Where's Sisi?"

A woman in her late sixties runs out from Lena's room, holding a pile of clothes in her arms. "Mikhail, I didn't hear you come in. I thought . . ."

She stops mid-sentence when she notices me, and her eyes widen.

"Sisi, this is my wife."

For a moment she appears slightly confused, looking from me to Mikhail, and back to me again, but then she collects herself.

"Oh, yes, of course. Mrs. Orlov, nice to meet you." She blinks at me again, then turns toward Mikhail. "Lunch is in the oven. Lena already ate, so I wanted to take her outside to play."

Mikhail nods, puts the girl down, and crouches in front of her. "Sisi will take you to the park. Go get your backpack."

"Okay." Lena runs to her room, only to return a few seconds later carrying a small glittery pink backpack with bunny ears. I watch her as she opens a shoe cupboard near the entrance, takes out a pair of small white sneakers, and sits on the floor to put them on. I have a cousin her age, and he wouldn't know how to put on his shoes by himself if his life depended on it. When she's done, she takes Sisi's hand, waves at us, and they leave.

I feel a light touch on my back and turn to find Mikhail holding a strand of my hair between his fingers.

"Let's sit down and you can ask your questions," he says and lets the strand fall away.

He leads me to the dining room table, unlocks his phone, and slides it across the wooden surface toward me. I look at him, then at the phone before taking it in my hand and starting to type. When I'm done, I slide the phone back to him.

He looks down at the screen.

"Lena's mother is gone," he says. "Lena wasn't planned. Her mother wanted an abortion. I said I'd kill her if she aborted my child, so after she gave birth, she left her with me, took the money I gave her, and walked away. A few months ago, I found out she overdosed on heroin."

I suck in my breath and stare at Mikhail. He's raised Lena since she was a baby. If he'd told me this before I saw her with him, I never would've believed him. He seems so closed off and unapproachable.

He looks down at the phone again, reading the next question.

"I tried explaining the situation to Lena, but I'm not sure how much of it she understood. She knows you'll be living with us from now on. She adapts well. I don't expect any problems."

His gaze finds mine and he watches me in silence for a few moments, and I find myself looking at his eye. It's the most unusual shade of blue, like clear ocean water.

"Will this be a problem for you? Me having a child?"

I lean back and raise my eyebrows at him. Why would it be a problem? I guess he reads the answer on my face because he nods and looks down at the phone again.

"Lena's daily schedule?" he asks and looks up, surprised.

I nod.

"She's up at seven. Sisi comes to take her to day care and brings her back home around three. They have lunch and go for a walk or to the park. Sisi is usually off around five, but she comes over to watch Lena in the evening when I have to work. Sometimes, when Sisi's granddaughters are staying with her, she takes Lena to her place for a sleepover. Like last night."

He places the phone on the table and nods toward it. "Any more questions?"

I shake my head.

"Let's eat then."

My strange husband goes to the kitchen and starts taking plates from the cupboard, and I stand up to help him.

I watch Bianca as she takes the plates and cutlery, carries them to the table, and comes back for the glasses. She took the fact that I have a child unexpectedly well, especially since I ambushed her with it instead of telling her in advance. The thing is, I wanted to see her reaction. It's not every day a person is forced to marry a stranger and learns afterward that their new spouse also has a child. I have no idea what I would've done if Bianca said she didn't like kids. Lena is the most important person in my life, and I hope the two of them will get along.

Bianca turns and reaches for the carafe with water, accidentally stumbling into me a little, and I go still for a second. It's easier when I am the one initiating the contact. I lean to the left, extending my hand as if to get the salad bowl, and let her hip brush my side. Nothing.

She turns and walks toward the table, carrying the water, and I follow her with my gaze, noticing the way her pants mold to her legs and her tight ass. Images of her naked in my bed, pinned down by my body, suddenly flood my mind. It's been so long since I've wanted to feel a woman's bare body next to mine, but now I do. And for someone with skin contact issues, that's a highly disturbing realization.

"I need you to write down your plans for the next two weeks," I say. "If you want to go somewhere, I'll take you. Or if I'm not available, one of my guys will go with you."

Bianca looks up from her plate and shakes her head.

"It's nonnegotiable. I don't know who was behind that shooting yesterday, or what they were trying to achieve. Please don't leave the apartment alone. Can I trust you on that, Bianca?"

She doesn't like it, I see it on her face, but she nods and goes back to her meal. I watch her secretly, her hands, her long blonde hair. Damn, I'm fascinated with that hair of hers. She braided it before lunch, and it now falls over her shoulder to her front. I dreamed about threading my fingers through those blonde waves last night.

The door behind me opens, and in the next moment, the sound of small feet thumping across the apartment reaches me.

"Hands, Lenochka," I say when she runs into the dining room.

"They're not dirty."

"You must wash your hands, zayka. Come on, say goodbye to Sisi and let's go to the bathroom."

I can't stop watching him.

It amazes me the way Mikhail interacts with his daughter. He never ignores her questions, no matter how silly they may seem. How affectionate he is with her. One of her pigtails came loose at some point this afternoon, and she asked him to fix it. I couldn't take my eyes off his huge hands as he carefully tied her hair. There's so much love in every single act.

They went into Lena's room some time ago, after she had dinner, and I now find myself drawn toward the door Mikhail left open, peeking inside. He's sitting on the edge of the bed, holding a big book with a princess on the cover, while Lena lies under the blanket. He's reading her a story. How can this be the same man who only this morning casually thrust a blade into my father's hand?

"Bianca!" Lena calls out when she sees me. "Come, Bianca. Daddy is reading a story."

I look up at Mikhail, waiting to see what he'll say. I don't want to intrude on their time. He watches me for a moment, then nods as I come to sit on the floor next to his legs and lean my back on the side of the bed. There are a few moments of silence and then he resumes reading. The story has something to do with a lost horse, but I don't pay attention to the plot because I'm too focused on the tone of his voice. Deep. A little raspy. I close my eyes and just listen.

I feel a light touch on my cheek—there one moment and gone the next. I keep my eyes closed, pretending I didn't notice it. A few moments pass, then I feel a tug on my hair as he removes the hair tie binding my braid, and the strands fall loose. Nothing else happens at first, and I wonder if that's all he planned to do. Then his fingers start combing through my hair. He's still reading but keeps playing with my hair, and I lean my head back into his touch. And his voice . . . it feels like a caress by itself. He has an accent, I realize. It's subtle, but it's there. I love it.

A finger skims over the sensitive spot at the back of my neck, and a slight shudder passes through my body. The hand in my hair stills, then vanishes. No, no, no . . . I lean my head back even more, hoping he'll get the memo. He does. There are a few slow strokes down the length of my hair, and then a brush of a finger at my temple. I'm not sure how much time passes, but when Mikhail finishes the story and removes his hand from my hair, my neck is stiff from keeping my head at such an unnatural angle for so long. It must have been at least twenty minutes.

"I have some work to finish," he says. "I'll be in my office if you need anything."

He stands up from the bed, walks around me to adjust the blanket around Lena's shoulders, and leaves the room. He's not a talkative person, that's for sure.

I look around the room, regarding the pale pink walls covered with images of animals and cartoon characters and the silky curtains embroidered with flowers. In the corner, there's a big dollhouse and two huge baskets overflowing with toys. I stand up and go to the dresser opposite the bed and look at the picture frames lining its surface. There's not enough light to see the details, but there are at least ten of them, and Lena is in each one. On the side, there's a big box with hair ties in a rainbow of colors. I find it hard to imagine Mikhail browsing in a store and shopping for pink curtains or the frilly cushions lining the wall on one side of the bed, but somehow, I know he's the one who bought them. Such an enigma, this husband of mine.

Chapter four

Mikhail

I'M BUTTONING LENA'S SWEATER WHEN I HEAR LIGHT steps approach and lift my head to find Bianca standing in the doorway. She looks around, walks to the dresser to take the box with Lena's hair ties, and turns toward me with a question in her eyes. I look at the box she's holding, then back to her face. Bianca sighs, points to the box, to herself, and then to Lena. She wants to do my daughter's hair, and the realization makes something in my chest squeeze.

"Lenochka, do you want Bianca to do your hair today?"

Lena's head snaps up and she beams. "Yes! I want lots of braids, like Noemi from day care. Bianca, Bianca, do you know how to make lots of braids? Daddy only knows pigtails."

Bianca's trying not to laugh at my daughter's babbling and fails terribly. She sits down on the bed next to me and motions for Lena to climb on her lap. I watch her as she takes a small strand and starts plaiting it into a thin braid, then moves to the next strand. She repeats the process until there are at least fifteen braids. It takes quite some time because Lena fidgets during the whole ordeal, turning around and picking different ties. Not once does Bianca snap at her. She just smiles, and shakes her head.

As soon as her hair is done, Lena jumps down from Bianca's lap and runs from the room, leaving the two of us sitting on the bed next to each other. I hear Sisi from somewhere in the living room, complimenting Lena's hair as my daughter continues babbling, but I don't move from my spot on the bed. Bianca's hand is right next to mine, and I can't resist the crazy compulsion to touch her again.

I reach out and place my hand over hers. "Thank you for doing Lena's hair." When I turn my head to look at her, she's watching me.

Our faces are only a few inches apart, and I wonder how a creature so painfully beautiful can bear to look at me and not flinch?

"I have to go check on something in one of the warehouses, but I'll be back in a couple of hours," I say. "If you want, you can invite your sister to come over, but clear it with the security guys downstairs. Just send them a message. I'll leave the alarm codes and the spare key card for the elevator and the door on the counter."

Bianca nods and her hand starts moving under mine, but instead of pulling away as I expect her to, she turns her palm upward and intertwines her fingers with mine.

"Daddy!"

I look down at our joined hands and then back at Bianca's face.

"Daddy! Daddy!"

Yeah, Lena always has the best timing.

"I have to go." I stand up and let Bianca's hand slip from mine. "If you need anything, message me."

She looks up, those whiskey-colored eyes regarding me with interest. I could spend hours gazing into Bianca's eyes.

"Okay," she mouths and stands from the bed. As she walks past me, she reaches over and brushes the back of my hand with hers.

Bianca

"Wow. Just . . . wow." Milene turns around in the middle of the living room and walks toward the tall windows overlooking the city. "The view is to die for."

I stand next to her, looking at the rooftops and sidewalks visible below.

"So . . . did you two, you know?"

"*What?*"

"Did you have sex?"

"*No.*"

"Renata told me her husband forced her to sleep with him the same night," she says. "Theirs was also an arranged marriage, but her husband didn't care about the fact they were basically strangers. He hurt her real bad, Bianca. I was so afraid the same would happen to you."

"*He gave me the guest room. And he hasn't tried anything so far.*"

"Do you want him to?"

"*Yes.*"

Milene stares at me, her eyes wide. "Are you serious?"

"Why? He's my husband. I am attracted to him."

"Attracted to him? Bianca, are you blind? He is . . ."

"He is what?"

"He is . . . he has only one eye, for God's sake, and you say you like him?"

"Yes, I like him. Do you have a problem with that?"

"No, I just . . . whoa. Did you ask what happened? To his face I mean."

"No. He'll tell me when he sees fit. I won't ask."

"And it doesn't bother you? The scars? The eyepatch?"

"No. I find Mikhail sexy as hell."

"You're out of your mind."

"Wait until you see him in the tight Henley he put on this morning. Hot. I bet he's even hotter without it."

"My God, you really like him. How is that possible? I mean . . . look at you. You could have had any man you wanted. You . . . you dumped Marcus, for crying out loud."

"Marcus is a spoiled idiot."

"Okay, but . . ." She stops mid-sentence and stares at something over my shoulder. "Is that . . . that's a child's room. Why is there a . . ."

I take her forearm to bring her attention back to me.

"Mikhail has a daughter."

"What? Did you know?"

"No."

"Okay, I'm telling Dad. There must be something he can do to annul the marriage."

"Don't you dare."

"Are you fucking serious? You're twenty-one and he expects you to raise his kid!"

"Lower your voice. He never said that, and believe me, he

doesn't need me to raise his daughter. He's doing that amazingly well himself. And I like Lena. She's a great kid."

"Bianca . . ."

"How is Father dearest doing? Mikhail stabbed him pretty hard, I hope his hand isn't too damaged."

Milene looks at me with horror in her eyes. "Your husband did that?"

"Father hit me again yesterday when I came to get my things. Mikhail wasn't pleased with that." I smile when I remember the look on my father's face as he stared at the letter opener lodged into his palm. *"It was very exciting to watch."*

"Okay, that's it. I'm calling Mom's psychiatrist. You need professional help."

"No, I don't think I do."

Milene went home hours ago, and Mikhail still isn't back. He messaged me around two p.m., saying Sisi will take Lena for a sleepover. He probably doesn't want to leave his kid with a stranger, although, I wouldn't have minded watching her.

It's almost midnight. Should I be worried or is this the standard occurrence? I have no idea what exactly his job is in the Bratva.

I take my phone and open the contact list. Should I message him to ask if everything is okay? Will it sound stupid? Yeah, it probably will. I don't want him to think I'm checking on him. Maybe I could ask something benign. If he replies, it means he's okay.

23:14 Bianca: Regarding my plans. I need to do

some shopping tomorrow. Also, I accepted an offer to teach a guest ballet lesson in the local ballet school on Thursday next week. It starts at nine a.m., and I should be done by midday.

23:22 Mikhail: I probably won't be back before tomorrow afternoon. I'll send Denis to pick you up at ten a.m. and take you shopping.

I read the message and feel an unexpected pang of disappointment. Apparently, I was secretly hoping I'd see him tonight. I start to place the phone on the table next to the bed, but then change my mind and type another message.

23:26 Bianca: Can I use the gym sometimes?

23:28 Mikhail: Of course. I'm usually done with my workout by nine a.m., so it's yours after that. Just one request—I don't like an audience when I'm working out, so please wait until I finish.

What a strange request. I'm pretty certain I'd enjoy watching Mikhail work out, but I'll respect his boundaries.

23:29 Bianca: Deal.

I put down the phone, turn off the light, and slide under the blanket when I hear the ping of an incoming message.

23:31 Mikhail: Can I take you to dinner on Friday?

An idiotic grin spreads across my face as I look at the screen. I feel like a teenage girl who just got invited on a date for the first time.

23:32 Bianca: Yes, you can.

Mikhail

I put my phone away, check the bandage on my arm, and turn toward the man tied spread-eagle to the wall.

"Now, where were we?" I ask as I take a knife from the metal table. I check its sharpness by holding it up to the light of the bare lightbulb, then stand in front of the bound man. He's already in a rough condition. To say he wasn't happy when Yuri and I ambushed him as he was leaving his girlfriend's house, would be an understatement.

"Oh, yes. You were going to tell me who paid you to send one of your gang members to my wedding, and who let the asshole in. That was a really stupid move."

The Albanian gang leader spits on the floor.

"One of the tough ones. Great." I walk back to the table, leave the knife, and pick up gardening scissors instead. "Let's start with the ears, then, and see where it leads us."

The door behind me opens with a squeak, but I remain sitting in my chair, watching small rivulets of blood trailing down the Albanian's arms, and then dripping one by one into a big puddle on the floor. There's a severed ear lying next to his right foot, and several teeth scattered around.

"Anything?" Yuri asks and places a cup of takeout coffee on the table.

"Someone hired him online," I say. "He never met the man who ordered the job. Everything was settled via phone.

The client wired twenty-five grand before the job, and twenty-five more right after it was done."

"Who was the target?"

"He doesn't know. The shooter was to meet the client before the wedding to receive details. The client is the one who arranged to get him inside the hotel."

"So, we have nothing so far." Yuri walks to stand in front of the gang leader and cocks his head to the side, inspecting my work. "Is he dead?"

"Just passed out." I grab the coffee, take a sip, and grimace. "I told you no sugar."

"Sorry," he mumbles and pokes the Albanian in the chest with his finger. The man stirs, lets out a strangled noise, then passes out again. "I've always admired how you manage to keep them alive for so long."

"Practice makes perfect, Yuri."

"Yeah. Remind me never to get on your bad side." He throws a look at me over his shoulder. "You're one scary motherfucker."

"No shit." I lean back in the chair and take another sip of coffee. It's awful. "Is Anton back?"

"Yeah. We caught another guy from the same gang. Anton has him in his truck. He might know something. How much time do you need to finish with this one?"

I put the coffee down and take the gun from the table. "Move away."

Yuri takes a step to the side. I aim and shoot the Albanian at the center of his head. "There. Finished. You can bring in the next one."

Chapter five

Bianca

Denis opens the car door for me and rushes to get my bags from the back seat. I try to take them from him, but he hastily moves them out of my reach.

"No. Boss would kill me." He shakes his head and starts walking toward the building's entrance.

I look at the heavens and follow him inside. It's just some cosmetic products and a few pieces of clothing, but he wouldn't let me touch the bags the whole morning, insisting on carrying them for me. Denis is a nice guy, somewhere around twenty-five, and from what he said, he's been working for Mikhail since he was eighteen. And he talks nonstop. He's already given me the short version of his childhood story, which wasn't a nice one, then a report on all the girls he's dated for the past six months. There were at least twenty of them. After that, he gave me a quick lesson on how to change a flat tire. He clearly has no problem with me not being able to contribute to the conversation, because he hasn't stopped babbling for two hours.

When we reach the top floor, Denis gives me the bags, at last, and leaves. I use the card to enter the apartment and stop dead at the threshold.

"I thought shopping trips lasted at least several hours," Mikhail says while standing in front of the kitchen sink, pressing a bloody rag to his forearm.

I let the bags fall on the floor, rush toward him, and look at everything he has lined on the counter—antiseptic spray, antibiotic cream, bandages, and a needle with a thread. Is he planning on sewing himself?

"Go to your room. I'll call you when I'm done."

I ignore him, turn on the water, and start scrubbing my hands with the soap.

"Bianca, leave."

There's something very dangerous in the tone of his voice, like he is angry at me for some reason, but underneath, there's something else. I can't quite define it.

Very slowly, I turn toward him and, without breaking eye contact, place my hand over his, which is still holding the bloody rag to his arm. He's looking down at me, his lips pressed together in a hard line, and his blue eye watches me with such intensity I get the impression he can see right into my soul.

Finally, his grip loosens, and he removes the rag. Only then do I notice he's in a T-shirt, something I've never seen him wear before. I look down at his forearm and it takes all my self-control not to show any reaction to what I see. The wound itself is not so bad, a few inches in length and not that deep. It looks like a knife wound. What's really bad is . . . everything else.

The inside of his forearm is badly burned, a long swath of mottled skin running diagonally from his wrist to the inside of his elbow. It looks like a very old scar, just like the others. Long thin lines crisscross his arm in different directions, probably wounds inflicted by the tip of a knife. I allow only a second to collect myself, then I take a package of sterile gauze and the antiseptic and start cleaning the gash.

"I see you've done this before," he says.

Without lifting my eyes from the gash, I hold up four fingers, throw the bloody compress into the sink, and take a new one. Angelo was an idiot when he was younger, always getting into fights, so I had a lot of experience dealing with the consequences of his moronic behavior.

After I repeat the cleaning process several times, I take the needle and start looking for the numbing spray among everything on the counter, but I can't find it. I look up and find Mikhail watching me. Damn, how can I explain this? I mimic the spraying motion and point toward his wound.

"You can sew it without it. It won't need more than two stitches."

He can't be serious.

"Just do it." He nods. "I have a high pain tolerance."

I look down at his arm, taking in the multitude of scars. Yes, he probably does. I take a deep breath, pinch the skin on each side of the cut, and start with the first stitch. Mikhail doesn't even tense when the needle pierces his skin. It's disturbing. After I'm done patching him up, I place a clean compress over the cut and bandage his forearm.

There's a light touch on my face, just above my cheekbone. It lasts just a moment and then he removes his finger.

"Thank you, solnyshko," he says and leaves the kitchen.

I take the meat casserole from the oven, put it onto the counter, and look toward Mikhail's bedroom. He went inside after I patched him up and hasn't come out since. He's probably sleeping. Where had he been the whole night? How did he get the knife wound? And what happened to his arm before to leave those scars? When it comes to my husband, I have a long list of questions and zero answers. Will it always be like this?

The front door opens, and Lena runs inside, giggling, with Sisi following. She'll wake Mikhail. I grab my phone from the counter, rush to Lena who's sitting on the floor taking off her shoes, and crouch in front of her. I brush her hand with mine and she looks up, smiling.

"Bianca, Bianca, I have a new drawing. Wanna see?"

I put a finger over my lips and point to Mikhail's bedroom. When she looks over and back at me, I put my palms together on my cheek to show a sleeping pose.

"You sleepy, Bianca?"

I sigh. Communicating with a small child is going to be hard without being able to speak, and she's too little to read. Taking my phone from the floor, I type a message and give it to Sisi, who's standing next to me and watching my interaction with Lena. She looks up from the screen and nods, a surprise visible on her face.

"Daddy is sleeping, Lena. We need to be quiet."

"Okay," Lena whispers.

"Bianca prepared lunch. She says if you're quiet and eat your lunch, she'll teach you ballet."

"Yes! Yes, Bianca. I'll be quiet. Do you really know ballet?"

I smile and nod, then put my finger on my lips again.

"Come, Lena." Sisi takes her hand. "Let's go change so you don't get food on your pretty dress."

While Sisi helps Lena change, I set the table for the three of us and tidy up the mess I made in the kitchen while preparing lunch. Sisi brings Lena back a few minutes later and the three us sit down to eat. During the meal, we have to remind Lena at least five more times to be quiet. As I watch Sisi with Lena, they seem to get along exceptionally well. A question comes to mind, so I take my phone, type, then show Sisi the screen.

"I've been working for Mikhail since Lena was a baby," she responds. "He hired me when Lena came to live with him. She was two weeks old."

My eyes widen. How did Mikhail manage with a baby so small, all by himself? Sisi couldn't be there twenty-four seven. I take the phone and type another question, then pass it to Sisi.

"Yes, it was hard. But Lena was a really good baby, she barely cried at all, and I came every day, but still . . ." She sighs. "I don't know how he pulled it off. During the first couple of months, he barely slept, but after Lena started sleeping through the night, it got easier. I offered to start taking her to day care during the day and stay with me overnight, but he declined. It took me a week to convince him to finally let her go when she was two. He loves her very much."

Yes. Anyone can see how much Mikhail adores his daughter. Especially someone like me, who was raised by parents like mine.

"Bianca, Bianca, can you show me ballet now?" Lena asks, swinging her legs forward and back.

I help her down from her chair, and taking her hand in mine, I lead the way into my room.

"Are you sure you don't want me to stay?" Sisi asks, but I just shake my head and raise my thumb up. I'll find a way to entertain Lena until Mikhail wakes up.

I take my phone from the nightstand and look at the time. Almost six in the evening. Shit. Looks like I'm getting too old for pulling two all-nighters in a row. Sisi's probably gone home already, which means Bianca is watching Lena. My daughter is a good kid, but she's a handful.

After a quick shower, I walk out of my bedroom, expecting to find the girls watching TV or something, but there's no one in the living room or anywhere around. The door to Lena's room is closed, and there's a faint sound of a children's song coming from inside. I open the door slightly to see what's going on, and my hand stills on the handle. With her back to the door, Bianca is standing in the middle of the room, her arms raised over her head. She has one of those fluffy white skirts on over her jeans and is wearing her ballet slippers. Next to her, Lena is in a similar position, standing on her toes and wearing one of Bianca's shorter stage skirts. It reaches almost Lena's feet.

Bianca lowers one of her hands, taps Lena on the back to straighten her spine, and starts rotating herself slowly until she sees me standing in the doorway. She smiles at me, and it feels like a ray of light on freezing cold skin.

"Daddy, Daddy, I'm a ballerina. See?"

I look down at Lena, who's twirling on the tips of her toes.

"I see, zayka."

"I want ballerina shoes like Bianca's. Please? Bianca, tell Daddy I need the shoes. I have the skirt, but I need the shoes."

I bend to scoop Lena into my arms, set her on my hip, and place a kiss on her head.

"We'll buy the shoes, Lenochka," I say and look at Bianca, who is sitting on the bed, removing her slippers. "I'm sorry. I fell asleep."

She cocks her head to the side, regarding me, then stands up and walks toward me. Leaving her slippers on Lena's dresser, she takes the hem of my left sleeve and starts carefully pulling it up. When she has the sleeve pulled up to my elbow, she inspects the bandage around my forearm. There's no blood, but it's wet from my shower. Bianca lets go of my arm, narrows her eyes at me, and heads into the kitchen.

"Daddy, can we watch Elsa on the big TV? Can we, Daddy?"

"Sure, zayka."

I take Lena to the living room, put on the movie, and sit down on the couch next to her. It must be the hundredth time I'm watching the thing, but Lena loves it. There's a sound of bare feet on the floor, and Bianca comes over and sits on the coffee table in front of me, holding the box with compresses and bandages I keep under the sink. She places the box on the table next to her and looks pointedly at my forearm until I extend my left arm. She removes the wet bandage and dressing, then gently cleans the cut and wraps a fresh bandage on it. I expect her to leave when she's done. Instead, she moves to sit on the couch next to me, curling her legs under her, and focuses on the movie.

Chapter
six

Bianca

I READ THE RECIPE ON MY PHONE, CHECKING THE ingredients lined up on the counter. There's flour and sugar in the cupboard, but I'm missing raisins and almonds. I also need more chocolate.

Yesterday, Lena said one of her friends brought cookies to the day care class, and she talked about them for twenty minutes, describing the different shapes and flavors. She asked Mikhail if he'd make her cookies, so she can take them to class as well. The look on his face was priceless. I imagined my huge husband making cookies, and barely managed to keep a straight face as he explained to Lena how he's not good at baking. I'm not much of a cook myself. I can make a few decent dishes and some sweets, but it's nothing epic. Most of my time growing up was reserved for ballet, but when I did have an hour or two free, I loved to go into the kitchen and help our cook prepare food. I never tried making cookies, but it can't be that hard. I grab my phone and send Mikhail a message.

14:17 Bianca: I need to run to the store. I'll be back in twenty.

A minute later the door to Mikhail's office opens. He walks out, comes over to the kitchen, and looks at everything I've set out on the counter. His gaze dances over the big pan I've lined with parchment paper, a bowl with grated chocolate, and a little pot with a huge chunk of butter I've left to melt.

"You're making cookies for Lena," he says and looks at me. I can't gauge the expression on his face, but he seems confused.

I shrug, type on my phone, and show him the screen.

Don't get your hopes up. It's my first time, so I don't know how edible these will turn out to be.

He places his finger on my chin and tilts my head up, his blue eye watching me. I find myself focusing on his lips. Hard, pressed together. Would they stay that way if I kissed him?

"Let's go to the store," he says and releases my chin.

My eyes follow him as he picks up his keys and wallet. He reminds me of a panther—big, black, and seemingly relaxed—but I have a feeling that underneath all that composure and calm, there is a beast.

The store near the apartment is tiny, but I manage to find everything I need, as well as a small set of cookie molds in various shapes and some colorful edible decorations. Mikhail has been following me in silence, always staying a step behind. When I stop in the fruit aisle and start putting some apples and bananas in the basket, he reaches to take it from my hand, and our fingers touch. I slowly let go of the handle, but make sure to brush the back of his fingers before I continue browsing the fruit.

Mikhail pays for my purchases and carries the bags to the apartment. After he places them on the kitchen counter, I expect him to go back to his work. Instead, he leans with his back against the cabinets, crossing his arms in front of him, and watches me as I wash my hands. I can feel his gaze on me the whole time I prepare the dough. Each time I catch him out of the corner of my eye, I have to reread the recipe. I find it hard to concentrate, knowing he's there, watching me, but it's not because I'm nervous. It's because I like it.

After I manage to finish the dough without messing up, I split it into two, place half on the countertop in front of me, the other a bit off to the right, and turn toward Mikhail. I point a finger to the second half of the dough, then at him, and raise an eyebrow. He cocks his head to the side, regarding me, and I think the corner of his lips curve slightly upward. Without breaking eye contact, he moves away from the counter and comes to stand on my right. A calming feeling overcomes me when he's near, which I find rather unusual. I'm not comfortable with people I don't know well. It's hard for me to communicate with them, and we usually end up in an awkward silence. Mikhail doesn't seem to mind the fact I can't speak, probably because he's not talkative himself, and the silence between us doesn't feel uncomfortable at all. Just the opposite.

I break eye contact and start working the dough in front of me, wondering what he'll do. Mikhail watches me for a minute or so, then places his hands on his piece of dough and copies my moves. He has beautiful hands. Big, strong with long fingers, and I can't help but wonder how it would feel to have those hands on me.

Peals of laughter accompany the opening of the front door. "Daddy, Daddy, what are you doing?" Lena rushes toward us while Sisi closes the door behind them. "Can I? Can I?"

"Hands first, Lena," Mikhail says and points with his head to the bathroom. "Then you can make cookies with us."

Lena laughs and runs to the bathroom. Sisi stands at the threshold, her eyes huge as she watches Mikhail working the dough. He certainly makes an interesting sight, so big and badass, with his eyepatch and his black shirt stretched over his wide shoulders. Especially with a speck of flour on the side of his chin. I lift my hand, intending to wipe it off, but the moment my fingers touch his skin, his body goes utterly still. He focuses intently on his hands buried in the dough in front of him. I brush some of the flour from his chin with my thumb and quickly pull my hand away. Did I cross some boundary?

"Daddy, Daddy!" Lena runs into the kitchen. "I'm ready! Can I have some, please?"

"Okay, zayka."

Mikhail leaves the dough, heads off to the dining room table and comes back with a chair. Placing it next to the counter, he helps Lena climb onto it, and slides his dough in front of her.

"I'll make a cake. With chocolate." She grins and looks over at me. "Do you like chocolate? Daddy doesn't like chocolate, but he will eat the cake if I make it. I love chocolate, but Daddy says it's bad for my teeth."

I nod, smiling. She brushes her hands on the front of her dress and reaches for the bowl.

"Oh, I got flour on my dress." She looks up at Mikhail. "Will it wash away?"

"It'll wash away, Lenochka. Don't worry."

"You have flour on your face, Daddy." Lena giggles, then proceeds to play with the dough.

Mikhail turns his gaze toward me, looks down at my hand on the work surface, then tilts his head to the side, offering me his chin. Slowly, I reach out and brush away the remnants of the flour using the back of my hand, taking slightly more time than necessary.

Chapter seven

Mikhail

The two guys sitting in the coffee shop have been ogling Bianca for almost a minute. I squeeze my hand into a fist and take a deep breath. If we make it through this shopping trip without me killing someone, I will be pleasantly surprised.

Lena's been pestering me about the ballet shoes for days, and I've finally caved and brought her to the mall. I asked Bianca to come with us because I have no clue where to buy ballet shoes—and because I want to spend more time with her.

Bad decision.

Bianca is an exceptionally beautiful woman, so this is somewhat expected. Having a man throw a look at her occasionally, I could stomach. Maybe. What I didn't expect was every single man in the mall staring at her, or how furious each of those stares would make me.

I turn my head to the right and observe my wife, who's currently crouching in front of a store window, pointing out sundresses to Lena. Bianca is wearing skinny jeans and a white sleeveless shirt tied around her neck. The white heels she has on definitely make her legs look amazing, but still, it's nothing provocative. I try to imagine how the men here would act if she'd worn a miniskirt, and almost snap. Not going there.

Her hair is loose and, with her crouching like that, the tips of her pale blonde tresses almost reach the ground. Lena says something and points to the dress on the right. Bianca tilts her head and all her hair slides from her back to the side, and a few locks end up touching the floor tiles. I bend and gather her hair with my left hand, lifting it off the floor. Bianca looks up at me, and then to my hand holding the silky strands. She smiles a little and goes back to pointing out dresses to Lena.

"The red one! Daddy, can we buy the red one?"

I look at my daughter and sigh. "You have more than twenty dresses, Lenochka."

"Please! Just this one, please Daddy? Bianca likes it. Bianca, do you like it?"

Bianca laughs in that silent way of hers and nods, looking at me over her shoulder. Women. Never enough clothes. "Okay, but just this one."

I follow behind them as we enter the store and navigate between the racks. Along the way, Bianca pulls out what seems like every dress available in Lena's size. She drops the heap of at least ten dresses on a stool, places Lena in front of a mirror next to it, and holds up the first dress in front of her. It's the red one Lena liked, and my daughter squeals in delight. Bianca looks over at me and I nod. She takes the next dress, a dark green one with black details, and places the hanger under Lena's chin. They make eye contact in the mirror, and Bianca looks at her with a comically disgusted face. Lena laughs and copies Bianca's expression.

They continue the process with each dress, having a great time, and I enjoy watching them. After they're done, Bianca turns to me and holds up not one, but four dresses, looking at me with sad puppy dog eyes. Of course, we end up buying all four.

When we exit the store, Lena runs toward the big fish tank in the window of a store across the way. Bianca and I hang back a few steps. Suddenly, I notice a man heading in our direction—early twenties, business suit, seems to be in a hurry—but the moment he sees Bianca, his stride slows. His eyebrows raise slightly as he checks her out.

The neural pathways in my brain must have snapped and rearranged themselves, because in that instant, I decide I'm done. My issues with skin contact can go fuck themselves. I grab Bianca's hand, pull her to my side, and wrap my arm around her. Not close enough. She's not close enough. I tighten my arm around her and stand with her back plastered to my front. The pressure in my chest eases. That will do. I don't need a shrink to interpret my actions. When a man has already lost all he's held dear, it's normal for him to become slightly unhinged and scared it may happen again.

The fancy guy looks up, his eyes widening upon seeing my murderous look. Yes, motherfucker. She's mine. He gulps, turns to the right, and enters the nearest store. Much better. I look down at Bianca to find her watching me with surprise, and I wonder if I should explain my erratic behavior. Then, the corner of her lips pulls up slightly, and as if nothing strange has happened, she resumes watching Lena follow a fish with her finger.

Bianca

I don't know what's happened, but something has gotten into Mikhail. Since the moment we met, he's been extremely distant, avoiding almost any kind of physical connection. Other than a few light touches and helping me into his car, he's rarely initiated contact. I even started wondering if something was wrong. Maybe he's decided to compensate for the past several days, because he hasn't let go of my hand for the last two hours. We went to a store to buy Lena's ballet slippers and checked out a few more stores along the way. At one point, Lena complained she was tired, so Mikhail scooped her up. He never let go of my hand as he carried her on his left hip, and my ovaries almost exploded as I stole glances of him holding Lena so naturally on his side.

"Do we need anything else?" he asks when we leave the bookstore we visited to buy a children's book for Lena.

He turns his head and looks at me, and for a moment, I wonder why. Then, I realize I'm on his blind side and he probably can't see my answer otherwise. I shake my head.

"Good. I'll call Sisi to come watch Lena this evening. I'm taking you to dinner. Is that okay?"

I smile and nod. Yes, it's more than okay.

Is it too much?

I turn to the side and inspect myself in the mirror. The

dress is long, with a slit on the side, and a modest neckline. It is, however, red. Maybe I should change.

Mikhail's voice comes from the other side of the door. "Are you ready?"

Looks like it's going to be the red dress after all.

I open the door to find Mikhail standing there. Based on the way he's staring at me, he likes what he sees, and it sends a small thrill rushing through me. I turn to grab the coat I left on the bed, but Mikhail takes it from my hands and holds it out for me. Always a gentleman, this dark husband of mine. I reach to sweep my locks out from under the coat, but he beats me to it, sliding his hands under my hair at the base of my neck and carefully lifting it out.

"You take my breath away," he whispers in my ear.

Chills run down my spine as he takes my hand and leads me out of the apartment.

We arrive at the restaurant and while we follow the *maître d'* to the table in the corner, people are staring at us. They are trying to be discreet, but they focus on Mikhail's eye patch and scars, then lower their gazes to our joined hands, surprise clearly written on their faces. It seems like Mikhail doesn't notice, or maybe he's just pretending he doesn't. I hate it for Mikhail's sake and pretend I don't notice their cold stares or hushed whispers.

When we are seated, I take the menu to see what they have, but everything is in French. I could pick something randomly, but there's a risk I'd get snails or something similarly disgusting. Instead, I put it down, move my chair next to Mikhail's, and look down at the menu he's holding. It's in French as well, but I assume he can read it since he brought us here.

Mikhail looks down at me, puts his arm at the back of my chair, and starts listing the dishes for me. I'm not particularly picky, so I take out my phone and quickly type.

You choose, just no snails or anything nasty like that.

I then leave the phone on the table in front of him.

While we wait for the food, the waiter brings us wine, placing the glasses on the right side of our plates. When he leaves, Mikhail takes his glass and moves it to the left.

I reach for my glass, brush the underside of his forearm lightly, and look up.

"It's okay," he says. "Almost healed."

I type on the phone again.

I never asked what happened.

I show him the screen and point to his forearm.

"We tracked the shooter to an Albanian gang and went to catch the leader in order to question him. He resisted."

Did you find out anything?

"No, but we will. It's just a matter of time."

I wonder what he'll do to those who ordered the shooting, and what exactly Mikhail's job is in the Bratva, but then again, I'm not sure I really want to know.

The waiter brings our food soon after. I have no idea what I'm eating. It tastes like pork in mushroom sauce and it's mouthwatering. Mikhail's dish looks like pork as well, cut in small slices and with heavy seasoning over it. It smells amazing, so I lean closer, prick one piece of meat with my fork, and stuff it into my mouth.

"You like it?" There is a barely visible smile on his lips, as if he's amused with me stealing his food.

He should smile more. I stab a piece of meat from my plate and lift the fork toward him, wondering what he'll do.

Mikhail looks at the fork, then to me and leans forward, taking the offering.

"Absolute perfection," he says while looking right at me, and I think he is not talking about food.

For a moment, I wonder if he's going to kiss me. The way he's looking at my lips makes my body hum with excitement, but then he looks the other way. Am I doing something wrong? I know he's attracted to me. I see how he looks at me when he thinks I'm not watching—like he wants to burn the clothes from my body with his eyes.

What the hell is going on in that head of yours, Mikhail?

Chapter eight

Mikhail

DIMITRI CALLS ON TUESDAY AFTERNOON TO TELL me we've hit another dead end with the Albanians, making the sour mood I've been in for days even worse. I stand up from my desk and walk to the wall of windows overlooking the sidewalk below.

After Sisi came to collect Lena for a sleepover, Bianca went into the gym, carrying her ballet shoes and her phone. A few minutes later, the soft sound of a classic melody reached my office. That was four hours ago. I've tried to ignore it and do some work, but images of her dancing keep popping into my head, and I can't concentrate on anything else.

I've also been trying to avoid her for the last two days, because every time I see her, I have this maddening urge to grab her, drag her to my bedroom, and fuck her senseless. Before I married her, I had sex regularly. Each of my partners knew my rules, the main one being no touching. But Bianca . . . I want to touch her everywhere.

I don't know if Bianca would be up for it. She looked so

shocked when she saw my arm. It lasted just a fraction of a second, and if I wasn't paying attention, I would have missed it because she collected herself right away. My chest and back are in a much worse state than my arms, and I have no idea how she'll react upon seeing them. She'll see me without a shirt eventually. Maybe I should start wearing T-shirts in front of her, let her see my arms better so she can be somewhat prepared. I take the hem of my shirt and pull it up to my chest, regarding the scarred skin and trying to imagine looking at it through her eyes. Nope, nothing can prepare her for that.

As bad as it is, my right eye is so much worse. That, she'll never see.

The music coming from the gym changes to a slow rock ballad, and I can't ignore the craving to see her dance one second more. At the gym door, I take care to be as quiet as possible as I open it and then lean onto the doorjamb to watch her. She's wearing black leggings and an oversized top that falls off one shoulder. Her hair is piled atop her head in a messy knot. Her feet are bare, the ballet slippers lying discarded next to the wall, as she glides across the room in a complicated set of steps and jumps. She finishes in a beautiful pirouette.

I wait for her to turn around, but for several minutes, she just stands there, looking at the wall in front of her with her hands pressed to her lower back. When she finally turns, her eyes are red, and tears are falling down her face. She flinches when she notices me, then quickly looks away and starts walking toward her ballet slippers. She winces every couple of steps, her right hand still pressed at her lower back. That's when it comes to me. The reason why her role in the shows got shorter over the last few months. Why she decided to leave the troupe. I remember the poster stating it was her last show. I thought it meant for the season. It didn't.

It takes me several large strides to reach her and scoop her in my arms. She doesn't resist, just hooks her arms around my neck and places her head on my shoulder, still facing me. The tears are still falling, but the expression on her face is strangely blank. If not for the tears and red eyes, no one would know she's crying. I carry her to the living room and sit down on the couch, holding her close to my chest. It's strange, how much I enjoy having her body pressed into mine. There is a folded blanket on the side, so I take it and cover her, tucking it around her chin and legs. She feels so small snuggled into me, like a kitten.

I don't know how long we sit like this. Probably close to an hour passes, because night starts falling and the room gets darker. She's so still, and I start to wonder if she's fallen asleep, but then her hand moves, tracing lines on my chest. At first, I think it's a random pattern, but then I notice the repetition of the shapes. She's drawing letters with her finger, and it takes me a few moments to catch up. It's not so hard, just two short words, but I still wait for her to repeat the pattern a few more times to be sure I caught it correctly.

I notice the exact moment Mikhail realizes what I'm drawing in his chest, because his body tenses. Just in case, I do it one more time and trace the letters.

K-I-S-S M-E

He doesn't do anything at first, but then I feel his finger caressing my cheek. I hook my hand around his neck and rise to a sitting position, straddling him. Only the outline of his face is visible in the darkness. Night has fallen outside, and none of the lights in the room are on. There's enough light coming through the window for me to see his head bending down, and the next moment, his lips crash onto mine.

It's not light or subdued, but claiming. His hands cradle my face. The skin of his palms is hard and calloused, but the way he holds me, as if I'm something precious, is heartbreaking. I bury my fingers in his hair and let myself be devoured by his sinful lips while a fire of desire consumes me. He breaks the kiss and starts trailing kisses down my chin, and I lean into him, feeling his hardness pressing into my core while my breath comes in short quick bursts. I reach for the hem of my top and take it off, then try to unclasp my bra, but my hands are shaking too much so I slip it off over my head.

"Are you sure, Bianca?" Mikhail whispers in my ear and then places a kiss on the side of my neck.

Is he crazy? I've been imagining this for days. I place my mouth on his chin and bite him lightly.

It's like he's been restraining himself up until this point, waiting for my confirmation. He jumps up from the couch with me in his arms and carries me toward his bedroom. All the while, I try my best to unbutton his shirt. I manage to undo the first two buttons, but there are at least five more, and I can't concentrate on undoing all of them. Instead, I thrust my hands into the opening, grab both sides of the shirt, and yank them apart with all my might. The material tears. Buttons spring free and fall to the floor.

Mikhail lies me down on the bed, pulls off my leggings and panties, and starts unbuttoning his pants. Too slow. I need him inside me now or I'll go mad. I stand up on the bed, and the moment his pants are off, I jump back into his arms and hook my legs around his waist.

I've never been this bold with a man before. Marcus once said I should get counseling because I was cold and unaffectionate. He was right. I'd never really enjoyed sex with him or others. For years, I thought something might be seriously wrong with me since none of my partners could turn me on. Sex being necessary for a relationship, I just went with it because it was expected, and faked the orgasm.

Frigid. I thought I was frigid. Apparently not, because I'm so wet if I could think rationally, I'd be embarrassed.

Holding me under my thighs, Mikhail turns around and presses my back onto the wall. He's saying something in Russian, and even though I don't understand a word, just hearing his rough voice in my ear makes my insides melt. God, I want to feel him inside of me so badly, my whole body is trembling.

"My little ballerina," he utters as he kisses my neck. "It would be much easier if you weren't so beautiful."

Mikhail positions himself and slowly lowers me onto his cock. He's not even halfway inside me, and I'm already spasming around his huge length. When he buries himself fully inside of me, I gasp and my body shudders. The feel of his hard cock inside me and the rough wall against my back brings me just to the brink of an orgasm as he stretches me in the best way possible.

He whispers foreign but seductive words in my ear while his big hands squeeze my butt cheeks. His lips kiss the sensitive spot on the side of my neck as he finally begins to move. With each thrust he seats himself further inside of me, hitting a spot no man has ever hit before. Slow at first, and then faster. I bury my nails into his skin as his thrusts increase in force, and I can feel my body begin to tingle with my impending orgasm. It's crazy. Intoxicating. The absolute destruction of my body and mind. He pounds into me like a man possessed, each slam of his hips into mine causing my back to hit the wall, stealing my breath. I come and Mikhail is right behind me.

I'm so spent I can't gather the strength to unwind my arms from Mikhail's neck, so I just tuck my face into the crook of his neck and let him carry me to the bed. The last things I remember before falling asleep are hushed words and a featherlight kiss in my hair.

I tug Bianca closer to me, marveling at the feel of having her finally in my arms as I watch her face illuminated by the moonlight. I trace the contour of her eyebrow with a finger, then her small nose and pouty lips. She is so beautiful, it fucking hurts. It feels like sacrilege to have her bound to someone like me, or have my bloodstained hands touching her—hands that have killed and maimed so many. She deserves better. A house with a picket fence and a carefree life with a normal man. An honest man who wouldn't have to lie to her or hide the bad things he does when he goes to "work." A man who would never come home covered in blood.

She deserves to be able to go to a restaurant without being stared at while people around her whisper to each other, discussing why the hell she's with someone like me. I grew accustomed to the stares and hushed whispers years ago. They don't bother me in the least. But I don't like Bianca being the subject of gossip. If I was a better man, I'd send her away, annul the marriage, and set her free. I guess I'm a bad man, though, because I don't plan on letting her go.

How am I going to tell her I've hidden the fact I know sign language? That instead of making her situation easier, I've only made it harder? How can I explain my selfishness? Will she hate me for it?

I won't lie to myself by thinking Bianca is attracted to me, I'm not delusional. She was in a bad place tonight. Vulnerable, probably lonely, and craving human contact. And I was the only one here. In the morning, she'll likely regret what happened between us, so I'll enjoy these stolen moments. It'll have to be enough. I put my head on the pillow behind hers, bury my face into her hair, and hold her even tighter.

Chapter nine

Bianca

The room I wake up in seems vaguely familiar. I sit up in the bed and look around. Mikhail's room. Me, in Mikhail's bed. I smile and fall back onto the pillows. God, just thinking about last night makes me want to run out of the room, find Mikhail, and drag him back to bed with me.

The clock on the nightstand shows seven a.m. Where is he? Did he seriously leave me here and go workout as he does every morning? You don't do that after giving a woman the best sex of her life the night before. Where's the cuddling? Showering together? The second round?

I get out of the bed, go to the closet on the opposite wall, and steal another of Mikhail's T-shirts. If I remember correctly, the housekeeper is coming to do a big clean today, and I don't want to flash her if she's early. When I exit the room, there's no one around. No housekeeper, and no trace of my husband. I proceed to the guest room to take a shower and wash my hair, then go to the kitchen to make some coffee.

I scroll through my phone while drinking the dark elixir and see three messages, one from Milene and two from Angelo, all from last night.

> **21:12 Milene:** What are you getting Nonna? Please tell me you're not buying her another hat.

Damn it. With all that's happened, I've completely forgot Nonna Giulia's birthday party.

I open a new message window and start typing a message to Mikhail.

> **07:29 Bianca:** I forgot my grandmother is having her 96th birthday next Sunday. I have to buy her a present.

I open Angelo's messages next.

> **23:44 Angelo:** DAD LET THEM MARRY YOU TO MIKHAIL ORLOV?!

> **23:45 Angelo:** Don't fuck with me Bianca! It's not funny.

I stare at the messages. Looks like Angelo knows Mikhail and is not a fan.

> **07:31 Bianca:** I'm not fucking with you. How do you know my husband?

The door to the gym opens and Mikhail walks out. Why is he wearing a long-sleeved shirt again? No one in their right mind wears long-sleeved shirts in June, and I know for certain he has at least twenty T-shirts, minus the two I stole. He comes into the kitchen and goes to the fridge without even looking at me.

"Sisi will be coming at around three with Lena, so if

you need anything, just text her a list and she'll buy it along the way." He takes a bottle of water, closes the fridge, then heads toward his bedroom. "We can buy the present for your grandmother on Friday if you want." He looks at me over his shoulder.

Seriously? No good morning kiss or anything? Well, screw him and his collected self. I'm done playing this hot and cold game. He wants to pretend nothing happened last night? No problem. I can do the same.

I nod and turn my attention back to my phone.

"But I want Bianca to come, too."

I put down the box with the spices I'm organizing and look at Lena. She's standing at the door with Mikhail crouching in front of her and zipping up her jacket.

"Bianca, Bianca, come with us. If you're good, Daddy will buy you a donut. He always buys me a donut if I'm good in the park."

Mikhail watches me for a few seconds, and when I don't make a move, he turns to Lena.

"Some other time, Lenochka. Bianca's busy."

Yeah, Bianca is busy with tidying an already impeccable kitchen, trying to distract herself from mulling over all possible explanations for her husband's strange behavior. I sigh, take my phone out and send a message to Mikhail.

> **17:13 Bianca:** I don't have a jacket. Most of my clothes for cold weather are still at my father's house.

I didn't expect the temperature to drop so much. Most of the boxes which Denis brought from my home had dresses, summer clothes, and the stage outfits I didn't want to leave behind. I only have my elegant coat here with me, and I planned on asking Milene to pack the rest of the clothes in my closet.

Mikhail's phone pings. He takes it from his jeans pocket, looks at the screen, then starts typing. My phone vibrates a second later. Really? I snort. We're less than ten feet apart and he messages me back?

> **17:14 Mikhail:** You can borrow one of my hoodies.

I look up and nod. While he goes to his bedroom, I put the spices back in the drawer and walk toward the door to put on my sneakers. Lena is jumping around me, babbling about donuts, when I feel Mikhail's hand on the small of my back and turn. He's holding a folded gray hoodie in his other hand. It looks like he does own something other than black clothes.

I put the hoodie on, then look down at myself. The hem almost reaches my knees. The sleeves are at least another hand's length beyond the tips of my fingers. I look up and find Mikhail watching me. He's trying really hard to keep his expression serious, but his lips are tightly pressed together. He crosses his arms, places his fist over his mouth, shakes his head, and then bursts out laughing. It's rich and throaty, and I can't take my eyes off him. He's so beautiful when he laughs.

"Hold out your arms," he says.

I raise them, and he rolls up the sleeves for me, the left one first and then the right. He's still smiling, and I want to kiss him again.

"Bianca, you look funny in Daddy's clothes." Lena giggles next to me.

There's a mirror on the left of the door, so I take a few steps and glance at my reflection. I look even more comical with the sleeves rolled up three times. Mikhail stands behind me, and our eyes lock in the mirror. He's not smiling anymore, and only watches our reflections for a few seconds before abruptly turning away.

"Do you want us to drop by a store first? To buy you something in your size?" he asks without looking at me and opens the door.

I think about it for a moment. Do I look like an idiot? Probably. Do I care? Nope. I turn, take Lena's hand, and start toward the elevator. Hopefully, it's not his favorite hoodie, because I am keeping it.

Mikhail

I've fucked something up, and I'm not sure what. Bianca's been mad at me since this morning for reasons I can't understand. I've spent the whole day trying to figure out what I've done wrong, and still have no clue. Although, it looks like the worst has passed, because when I took her hand as we were leaving the building, she didn't pull away. She did, however, gift me a pointed look through narrowed eyes.

Sitting on the bench at the edge of the playground, I watch Bianca as she chases Lena around the sandbox. They've been fooling around for an hour. First at the slide, and then in the small children's playhouse, where Lena prepared a make-believe lunch out of leaves and rocks she collected. Bianca pretended to eat them. My wife looks even younger in my several-sizes-too-big hoodie, and for a moment, I feel a pang of guilt. What if Roman was right? Maybe I should've let Kostya have her. He's closer to her in age, so she'd probably have more things to talk to him about than with me. I don't talk much anyway. The two of them would have been much more suited as a couple.

I can't stop thinking about the moment before we left my place, when I stood behind her and saw our reflections in the mirror. Bianca, even wearing that ridiculously large hoodie, appeared so beautiful and sophisticated. And then there was me, looming over her like a hideous monster. I knew we were a bad match, but up until that moment, I didn't grasp how much.

"Daddy, Daddy!" Lena shouts and motions with her hand at me. "Come, Daddy!"

I stand up and walk toward the sandbox. "What is it, Lenochka?"

"You are the wolf now, Daddy. You chase. Me and Bianca will run away." She giggles and dashes toward the other end of the playground.

I turn to Bianca who's standing a few paces away, watching me with a question in her eyes. I take a few steps until I'm in front of her, bend, and whisper in her ear. "Run, my little lamb."

She tilts her head up at me, her lips widening in a mischievous smile, then turns on her heel and runs to Lena, who's hiding behind the slide. I take the first few strides in their direction, and when Lena sees me coming, she yelps and dashes to the left, giggling. I run after her. It takes me less than ten seconds to get to her, and she squeals in delight as I scoop her around her middle. I place a kiss on her cheek, then hold her under my left arm and turn toward Bianca.

There's a smug expression on her face as she watches me, but it transforms to surprise when I run toward her with Lena laughing madly under my arm.

"Faster, Daddy!"

Bianca dashes toward the playhouse on the other side, and she's rather fast. However, I'm faster and my strides are much larger. I catch up with her just a few feet from the playhouse, grab her around her waist with my free arm, and pull her against me. She's laughing. I can't hear it, but I can feel the way her chest moves under my arm. I lift her from the ground and carry them both to the small coffee shop opposite the park.

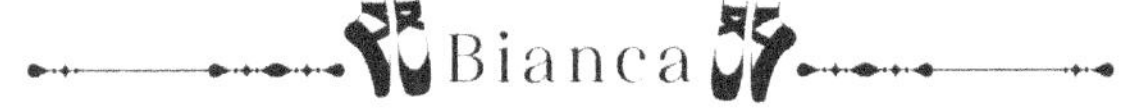

Bianca

I am still laughing as the double sliding doors open and Mikhail carries us into the coffee shop. A few people around the room look up at us in surprise. An older couple sitting by the window smiles and turns back to their drinks and pastries. On the other side of the store, a middle-aged woman sitting with another lady gawks at Mikhail's face without shame, then nudges her friend with her elbow and tips her head in our direction. The nerve some people have.

Mikhail lets me down, and taking my hand in his, walks toward the cash register.

"Black coffee?" he asks, and I nod. He's remembered I drink my coffee black.

"Daddy, I have to pee," Lena whispers.

"Just a second, Lenochka."

Mikhail orders a coffee for me and orange juice for Lena, tells the cashier we'll have them to go, then hands me his wallet. "I have to take Lena to the bathroom."

Holding the wallet in one hand, I point to myself with my free one, offering to take Lena, but Mikhail shakes his head.

"It's okay. I'll take her," he says and leads Lena toward the restrooms.

I pull out enough dollar bills for amount shown on the register and look up to find the guy on the other side watching me while he's pouring the coffee. He casts a glance toward the bathroom, where Mikhail just went to with Lena, then back to me and smiles. I don't reciprocate.

"Your dad is a really scary guy," he says.

I roll my eyes. Seriously? Mikhail might seem a few years older than thirty-one at first glance because of the eyepatch and scars, but it's more than evident he can't be my father.

"You think he'd let me take you to a movie or something?" The barista leans forward and winks.

Is this guy for real? He's barely seventeen, if that. Idiot. I place the money on the counter and turn just as Mikhail and Lena exit the restrooms. I size him up, noting the way his black jeans fit him perfectly, and how his black sweater molds to his rock-hard chest and stomach, remembering how it felt to be pinned against the wall by his magnificent body last night.

"Ready to go?" Mikhail asks when he arrives at my side.

I smirk, take Lena's juice from the counter and give it to her with the straw. Then, I place my hand on Mikhail's chest, and collecting a handful of fabric between my fingers, pull on his sweater. His face is expressionless, but I catch slight confusion in his eye as he bends down. When his face stops a few inches above mine, I raise on my toes and press my lips to his.

It was meant to be a quick kiss, but the moment I feel his mouth on mine, all reason flies out the window. The next thing I know, I'm clutching the back of Mikhail's neck while he crushes me against his body. My feet dangle above the ground, and we're kissing like there's no tomorrow.

"Yucky!" I hear Lena exclaim and my eyes snap open.

One impossibly blue eye is regarding me with such intensity that, for a moment, it feels hard to draw breath. I don't remember anyone looking at me like that, ever.

"Ty luch solntsa v pasmurnyy den', Bianca," he says into my lips, kisses me again, and slowly lowers me to the ground.

It feels like I've just run a mile, because my heart is thumping in my chest like crazy. I take a deep breath and turn to take my coffee from the counter. The barista is staring at me, his eyes wide.

"Eyes off my wife, kid," Mikhail says behind me.

The guy blinks, looks up at Mikhail, then takes a step back.

"Daddy, can we go buy donuts now? Can we Daddy?"

"Sure, zayka." Mikhail bends to scoop Lena up, takes my hand, and leads us toward the exit.

Mikhail

My phone starts ringing just as we enter the apartment.

"Wash your hands, Lenochka." I point to the paper bag

holding her donut, which she's clutching to her chest. "And dinner first. You can eat the donut after. Okay?"

"Okay, Daddy!"

I pull out the phone, look at the screen, and turn to Bianca. "It's Roman. Can you help Lena? I have to take this."

She nods, brushes her hand down my forearm, and hurries toward the bathroom. I still find it hard to process how much I enjoy her touching me.

"Pakhan?" I say into the phone.

"I need you to check on Sergei," he says. "He hasn't been answering his phone since this morning, and he has a meeting with Mendoza's men tonight. If he isn't in shape to take it, I need you to go instead."

"I'll be there in an hour."

I put the phone away and go to the bathroom where Bianca is helping Lena dry her hands.

"I have to go." I reach out and remove a strand of hair from her cheek. "I'll call Sisi to come and watch Lena. I don't know how long it'll take."

Bianca looks up at me, shakes her head, points to her chest, and then to Lena.

"You sure?"

She nods and takes Lena's hand.

"Lenochka." I bend and brush her chin with my thumb. "Daddy needs to go to work. Bianca will stay with you, okay?"

"Okay, Daddy." She beams and turns to Bianca. "Bianca, can we have a pajama party. Can we please?"

"Dinner first, zayka. And be good."

"Yes, Daddy." She takes Bianca's hand and starts pulling her. "Come on Bianca. Dinner first, then donut, then pajama party."

Bianca lets Lena lead her out of the bathroom and toward the kitchen. I follow them with my gaze, then head into my bedroom to change in case I have to go to the meeting later.

On my way out, I take a small detour to the kitchen where the girls are sitting at the breakfast bar, making sandwiches.

"Listen to Bianca," I tell Lena and place a kiss at the top of her head.

When I look up, I find Bianca watching me. God, I want to crush my mouth to hers so badly, but I don't dare. I have no idea what happened in the coffee shop earlier to urge her to kiss me, and I don't want to push her. It can't be easy for her, so instead, I just brush my finger down her cheek.

"Message me if you have any problems with Lena," I say and turn to leave.

When I'm at the door, I glance back and find Bianca watching me with narrowed eyes. I might be wrong, but it looks like she's mad at me again.

As I'm starting the car and wondering what the fuck I'm going to find when I get to Sergei's place, I hear my phone ping with an incoming message.

19:31 Bianca: You haven't eaten.

I stare at the message. I haven't. And she noticed.

19:32 Mikhail: I'll grab something along the way.

19:32 Bianca: We'll prepare a sandwich for you and leave it in the fridge. Just in case.

19:33 Mikhail: Thank you.

I leave the phone on the dash and drive out of the garage. Somewhere along the way, I hear another message arrive, but I don't open it until I park in front of Sergei's house. When I do, I sit behind the wheel for five minutes, staring at her message.

19:52 Bianca: From now on, I expect a goodbye kiss too. Please keep that in mind, Mikhail.

After dinner and a quick bath, I tuck Lena into bed and cover her with her flowery blanket.

"Bianca, Bianca, can I have a story? Please, Bianca."

I take my phone, browse for the online channel that has children's stories, and lie down on the bed with her. God, she looks so much like Mikhail, I wonder if there's even one feature she has from her mother. Maybe her nose, it's very tiny. I reach out to arrange her blanket better.

She turns to me. "Daddy likes you."

I smile and brush her cheek. She can't know that. Even I'm not sure what to think about Mikhail's behavior.

"Daddy kissed you. And he held your hand. I think Daddy really, really likes you, Bianca. Daddy doesn't like to touch people."

My hand on Lena's cheek freezes, my whole body going still.

"I like you, too, Bianca. Do you like me?"

I brush her cheek again and nod.

"Bianca, why can't you speak? Did you hurt your mouth? My daddy hurt his eye. Noemi says my daddy has only one eye but she's lying. Daddy has two eyes. I asked and he showed me. Noemi says my daddy is ugly. Is Daddy ugly, Bianca?"

My breath catches. I place my hands on either side of Lena's face, shake my head and mouth, "No."

"Daddy says he is a little ugly. I asked him. But you are so pretty, Bianca. You are like a princess. I like your hair. Will my hair be long like yours?"

Lena switches to telling me about what happened in day care the other day, something about a toy truck one of the boys broke, making the other boy cry, but I find it hard to focus. There was one sentence Mikhail said last night. It slipped my mind at that moment because I was too absorbed with his kisses. Something about how it would be easier if I was not so pretty.

Oh God. I close my eyes and shake my head. The long sleeves, the distance he's been keeping, all those hot and cold signals . . . Things make much more sense now.

"Sergei!" I hit the door with my palm a third time. "If you don't open this door, I'm going to break it down."

The alarm buzzes and the lock clicks. I grab the handle, open the door and step inside.

"Don't you dare shoot at me!" I yell into the empty living room. "And rein in that beast of yours."

"You can't break a reinforced door that costs more than

a car, dickhead." I hear Sergei's voice from the kitchen and head that way, then stop in my tracks at the threshold.

Sergei is sitting at the table in the middle of the kitchen, with a disassembled sniper rifle in front of him, polishing one of its parts and whistling. The whole surface of the six-seat table is piled with weapons of various kinds. Guns, knives, automatic and semiautomatic rifles, and God knows what else.

A few feet away, on a folded blanket next to the wall, lies a black dog the size of a small calf. It watches me for a few moments, then looks up at Sergei and goes back to sleep.

I take the phone from my pocket and call Roman.

"When and where is the meeting with the Mexicans?" I ask the moment he takes the call.

"They'll be at Ural around eleven."

I look at my watch. Half past eight. "It will probably be me going to the meeting. Let Pavel know."

"Fuck! How is he?"

"I just got here. I'll call you later." I cut the call and take a seat across from Sergei.

"Pakhan sent you?" he asks without looking at me and continues to polish the rifle part.

"Yes. You weren't answering your phone. He worries." I nod toward the table. "Doing inventory?"

"Kind of. Can't sleep." He places the polished piece into a box sitting at his feet and which contains the rest of the sniper rifle parts, and closes the lid.

"Since when?"

"I stopped counting. Three days. Maybe four."

"Jesus, Sergei." I shake my head. "Have you been eating?"

"I think so, yeah. I have some cans in the pantry."

I turn around, looking for his seventy-year-old butler-gardener-cook. "Where's Felix?"

"I sent Albert to a hotel for a week."

Ever since I've known Sergei, he's never called Felix by his actual name. It's always Albert. I have no idea what the deal is with the two of them, but Felix has been living in a small apartment above the garage since Sergei bought the house and joined the Bratva four years ago.

"Why send him away?" I ask.

"He was getting on my nerves. I was afraid I might kill him by accident." He snorts, reaches for the gun closest to him, and starts disassembling it.

"Maybe you should go visit a shrink?"

He looks up at me, leans back in his chair, and crosses his arms. "For the shrink thing to work, Mikhail, you need to actually talk to the guy about the things troubling you. For most of the things that annoy me, I signed documents saying I'd keep my mouth shut or end up in jail. Or worse."

The most dangerous thing about Sergei is most of the time he doesn't look crazy at all. His eyes are clear, his movements controlled, his voice steady, and to someone watching from the outside, he seems like a perfectly balanced person. Until he starts killing people. Even now, if it wasn't for the weapons scattered around the table, the only thing anyone would see is a clean-cut guy in his late twenties. Relaxed. Just chatting away as if nothing is bothering him.

"What about sleeping pills?" I ask.

"Don't you think I already tried those?" He sighs and resumes cleaning the gun. "It doesn't work. Nothing fucking works."

"Have you considered quitting? Leaving the Bratva and going to some deserted island or whatever?"

"Yeah, it wouldn't do it for me. Without work, I'd probably flip completely."

And God save us all if that ever happens. If Sergei does flip at some point, someone will have to put him down like a rabid dog.

"How about swapping with Pavel? You could take the clubs. Less stress there."

He looks up at me and bursts out laughing. "Can you imagine our polished put-together Pavel negotiating with Mendoza? Don't get me wrong, Pavel does a great job with the clubs, but Mendoza would eat him alive. We'd lose millions."

We probably would. I still find it hard to understand, but Sergei is exceptionally good at what he does. It seems in order to do good business with unhinged people, you need to have your own lunatic who speaks their kind of crazy.

"And what about the meeting with his men tonight?" I ask. "Can you handle that, or should I go instead?"

He looks up at me and smiles. "You hate meetings."

"Yeah, well, Pakhan's orders." I shrug. "So?"

"It would be best if you go. I'm not sure how much crap my sleep-deprived brain can deal with at the moment. Roman doesn't like my way of showing displeasure."

"Like trying to cut off Shevchenko's hand when he asked for better terms?"

"What he asked for was a steal." He reaches under the

table, takes out a big metal heavy-looking box that looks rather heavy, and places it on the table. "Do you know what they do to thieves in some countries? They cut off their hands. I like that practice."

Why am I not even slightly surprised? I look at my watch. "I better go then."

Sergei nods. "Don't let them lead you on. We've already set up the rates and quantities for this quarter, I'll text you the numbers."

"All right." I stand up. "Call me if you need anything. And please start taking Roman's calls."

"Sure." He shrugs, opens the lid of the box, and takes out something resembling a small grenade launcher.

"You don't have a tank hidden in the garage, do you?"

"A tank? Why the fuck would I keep a tank in the garage?"

"No reason. I was just wondering."

"If you need a tank, I can ask Luca. He has the best shit."

"Luca Rossi?" I look at him. "If Roman finds out you're buying guns from the Italians, it won't end well. You know we agreed on exclusivity for weapons purchases with Dushku."

"I can buy my personal guns from whomever I want, Mikhail." He smirks. "But it would be best if Roman doesn't find out. He'll probably throw a fit, you know what a drama queen my brother is."

I shake my head. "Call me if you need anything."

"I will. Let me know if you change your mind about that tank."

When I get back to my car, I call Sisi, then Denis, and then send a message to Bianca.

> **21:19 Mikhail:** I don't know when I'm coming back, probably in the morning. Sisi will come early to help Lena prepare for day care. Denis will take you to your ballet class after he drops them off. I'll be waiting for you when you are done. Just text me the address.

Afterward, I call Roman to update him on Sergei, put the phone on the dash, start the car, and curse. The only thing I hate more than business negotiations with our suppliers is clubs.

Chapter Ten

Bianca

When I exit the school building around noon, Mikhail is already waiting for me by his monstrous SUV. He's leaning on the hood with his arms crossed in front of his chest, looking mean and sexy in his all-black outfit and aviator glasses. His casual posture says he doesn't have a care in the world, but I'm not fooled. He's aware of everything happening around him. I've noticed how he scans his surroundings every time he arrives somewhere, weighing all possible threats in the vicinity. It's as if he is always expecting someone to jump out of the bushes and start shooting.

"How was the class?" he asks when I approach.

I don't intend to discuss the fact the class went well, or that they asked me to come again next week. Mikhail owes me something from last night, and I plan on taking it. I stop in front of him, cock my head, and regard him through narrowed eyes.

"Is something wrong, Bianca?"

I nod. It certainly is. Raising my hand in front of me, I curl my finger, asking him to bend down. Mikhail lowers his head. I wish he wasn't wearing those sunglasses, because even without them, it's hard to read him. I focus my gaze on his lips, still a couple of inches from mine, and see them curve up slightly. His hand cups my chin, and in the next moment, he crashes his mouth to mine.

It's not a soft kiss, but a raw, hungry one. He's always so perfectly controlled, but the few times his composure has slipped have me wondering what lurks below. I can't wait for the moment when the reins on his control snap completely.

He lets go of my chin but doesn't move away. "And now? Something still wrong?"

I smirk and shake my head. He's learning. I place my hand on his face, but the moment my fingers touch the skin of his right cheek, he lifts his head abruptly and steps back.

"We should go if we want to avoid traffic," he says and opens the passenger door for me.

We're halfway to the apartment when Mikhail takes out his phone and calls someone. He's speaking Russian again, and the only words I catch are "Ford Explorer". The person on the other end says something, and then Mikhail cuts the call.

"We're taking a small detour," he says.

We keep a steady pace, driving for about twenty minutes. Soon enough, we leave the hustle and bustle of the city traffic behind, and there are fewer buildings fronting the highway. We're heading somewhere out of town. Suddenly, Mikhail floors the gas pedal. I grab the door handle and hold on as if my life depends on it. The speedometer on the dash starts climbing, fast, reaching almost one hundred miles per hour. Mikhail looks in the rearview mirror and makes a sharp right turn, taking a narrow dirt road. I look behind at the black Ford Explorer taking the same turn and speeding after us. Mikhail keeps driving, maintaining the distance for twenty more minutes, then turns onto another dirt road leading to a factory visible in the distance. His phone rings once, then stops.

"Take my phone," he says. "Send a message to Denis. It's the number I just called."

I grab the phone, find the call in the log, and open a message window.

"Type… 'I need one of them alive.'"

I tense, my fingers freezing above the keyboard for a second, then type the message and send it.

"Now, listen to me carefully," he says, glancing at the rearview mirror again. "I'll park in front of the factory. You lock yourself in, get down onto the floor, and don't leave the car. No matter what. Do you understand?"

I nod and try to control the panic building in my chest.

"If things go south, you start the car and leave. Go downtown, park somewhere crowded, and wait. Someone will come and pick you up as soon as possible. The car has GPS tracking."

And leave him in the middle of nowhere? Is he insane? How will he get back?

"Do you understand what I'm saying, solnyshko?"

I don't plan on leaving him, but it's not the best moment to have that discussion, so I nod.

"Good."

The car screeches to a stop in front of the factory entrance. Mikhail takes off his sunglasses, reaches under his seat, and takes out a gun.

"Lock yourself in."

He jumps out and slams the door closed behind him, and then he's gone.

I run inside the abandoned factory, cock the gun, and stand by the broken window, which gives me a direct view of the road and the entrance gate. The vehicle following us rushes through the gate a moment later and stops about five yards from my car. No one gets out for a couple of minutes. They're probably debating what to do. Eventually, one of the back doors opens and a man gets out, holding a gun at the ready. He aims for the back window of my car, and shoots. Nothing happens, so he tries three more times.

It's an armored car, you idiot.

I throw a quick look toward the gate. Where the fuck is Denis? If I start shooting, they might hightail it out of here, and we'll lose them.

The other back door opens and a bald man in his forties gets out, carrying a shotgun. Fuck! I'm not sure how many rounds the glass can take, but I don't plan on risking Bianca's life. I aim at the bald guy's head, visible above the car door, and shoot. His head jerks backward and he crumbles to the ground at the same moment I kill the second guy. There are a few seconds of silence, then the two front doors open. I duck before the driver and another guy open fire in my direction.

Glass from the window starts raining down on top of me. One of the larger pieces embeds itself into my back, up by my shoulder. I reach back and take it out, slicing my hand in the process.

There's a sound of an engine roaring, and for a second, I think Denis has finally arrived. But the sound is too close. A second later there's a crushing sound and the gunfire ceases. I look through the window and shake my head. My sophisticated little wife has just rammed the pursuers' vehicle.

I rush out of the building and run toward the shooters, who are lying on the ground. Their doors must have been open when Bianca hit them. It seems the driver is more or less unscathed and is already reaching for the gun on the ground a few feet from him. I shoot him in the head before he gets to it, collect the gun, and circle the car. The last guy is crouched on the ground, vomiting. Based on the amount of blood at the back of his head, he hit it pretty hard. I kick his gun away from him when I hear the sound of another car approaching. Five seconds later, Denis parks behind me and jumps out.

"I see you have everything already handled, boss." He smiles like an idiot.

"Where the fuck were you?"

"I took a wrong turn. Sorry, boss."

I curse and point to the other three bodies. "Check them. Then call for a cleanup." I turn toward the vomiting guy. "Bag this one and take him to the east warehouse. I'll question him tomorrow. Call the doc in to see him, if necessary. I need him alive."

I turn around and head off toward my car.

Bianca

The first thing my husband says when he opens the door after I just saved his life?

"You smashed my taillights."

I raise my eyebrows, snort, and move over into the passenger's seat. Mikhail gets in, and when he reaches to turn on the car, I notice the blood on his right hand. I suck in a sharp breath and place my hand over his. He lets go of the keys and lets me inspect his palm. There's dirt mixed with the blood. I can't see where he's bleeding from, and I don't want to risk making it worse by trying to brush the dirt away. I take the hem of my T-shirt, tear a piece of the material, and then carefully wrap it around his hand. When I look up, I find him watching me. I point to myself, then to the wheel.

"It's just a scratch, Bianca. I can drive," he says and starts the car.

Mikhail spends the entire trip back to his place talking to someone over speakerphone. I'm not sure who it is, but the voice is familiar, probably their pakhan. I have no idea what's said because the whole conversation happens in Russian, so I lean back in my seat and close my eyes.

I've been shot at. Again. In less than a month. Will this become the norm for me now? Being married into the Bratva seems to be much more life-threatening than I expected. So why the hell am I not more shaken by this fact? I open my eyes just a sliver and watch my husband. There's something incredibly sexy in the way Mikhail speaks Russian, he sounds less guarded. I don't know if it's because he's using his native language or because he's close with Petrov. Will he ever be as relaxed with me?

Mikhail parks the car in the underground garage, and when he leans to open his door, I notice a red stain on the beige leather seat. He's hurt. Why hasn't he said anything, damn it? I follow him with my eyes and spot a wet stain on his shirt, near his left shoulder blade. What the fuck is wrong with him? I jump from my seat, slam the car door, and look up at him.

"Mad at me again?"

I point to his shoulder and throw my hands in the air. Of course, I'm mad!

"It's nothing, Bianca. Relax."

Relax? He's bleeding all over the place and he wants me to relax? I turn and start marching toward the elevator.

When we get inside the apartment, I go straight to the kitchen, open the bottom drawer where I stored the first aid kit the previous time, and start taking out the supplies. Mikhail watches me from the doorway, while I line up everything up on the kitchen counter, then scrub my hands clean. Once I finish, I turn toward him and wait.

Mikhail remains standing on the same spot, staring back at me, and I swear, if he doesn't come here this second, I'm going to drag him over myself. Finally, he moves and goes straight to the sink. After he removes my makeshift bandage and washes away the blood, he puts his hand on the counter in front of me, palm up.

Three of his fingers have been cut, probably with glass, but it's rather shallow. I clean the cuts, apply some antibiotic cream, and put a Band-Aid on each. I close the box, point to his shoulder, indicating with my finger for him to turn around.

"No. I'll handle that one."

And how does he plan to treat the wound on his back himself? I cock my head to the side and mouth the words to him, "The shoulder."

He ignores me and reaches for the antiseptic spray. Oh, for God's sake, he's so damn stubborn. I place my hand over his and press my other hand to his chest. Slowly, I trace the letters on his chest with the tip of my finger.

P-L-E-A-S-E

He watches my finger, then meets my eyes and there is a look on his face . . . I can't quite define it, but it seems vulnerable.

"Okay," he says, and grabbing me around the waist, he lifts me to sit on the countertop.

For a few moments he just stands there—his hands gripping the edge of the counter on either side of me, his body leaning forward, and his jaw set in a hard line. Our faces are so close, I can feel his breath on my skin while the deep blue of his eye watches me closely.

"It's not a pretty sight, Bianca," Mikhail says in an even voice, his face closed off. "If you can't stomach it, just say so."

I don't have a problem with blood. He knows that already. I'm missing something. Mikhail turns his back to me and starts unbuttoning his shirt. A feeling of dread collects in my stomach. I remember his arm from the one time I saw it. He always wears long sleeves, and the other night when I placed my hands on his back, I felt ridges on his skin. Although, it was too dark to see anything. His hesitation isn't about the wound at all. He doesn't want me to see his back.

Mikhail finishes unbuttoning his shirt, takes it off, and throws it onto the floor. I stare at his back as tears start pooling at the corners of my eyes, and no amount of self-control can keep them from falling. Long, slightly raised but faded with age marks crisscross his torso. Old wounds. So… so many of them. There are a few patches of untouched skin, but other than that, his whole back is a tapestry of scar tissue.

I close my eyes for a second and brush off the tears with my hand. When I look again, Mikhail is still standing in the same position, his back to me, looking straight ahead and letting me take my fill. I take a deep breath, reach for the compress pack and the antiseptic spray, and turn my attention to the cut on his left shoulder blade. It's not very deep and probably won't need stitches. I clean the cut with sterile gauze several times, coat the cut with antibiotic cream, then place butterfly bandages to hold the skin together. When I've finished, I put a layer of gauze over the wound and secure it with a few pieces of medical tape. I take another breath to prepare myself for the pain that will come and place my hand on his upper arm.

"Turn around, Mikhail." My voice is so faint, barely a whisper, but it feels like I'm yelling because my throat hurts like someone is scouring sandpaper over my vocal cords.

Mikhail turns to face me, and the movement is so quick and sudden, I flinch. He's looking at me like I've grown another head. I move my gaze down to his chest. No whip marks here, but there are burns on his side and stomach, as well as numerous scars from knife cuts, like those on his arms. Dear God, how is he even alive?

I look up at his closed-off face, raise my hands and bury them in his hair. Without removing my eyes from his, I hook one finger under the string of his eyepatch and wait. He doesn't say a word, just grinds his teeth and nods. I nod in reply and remove the patch.

He still has both eyes, but while his left eye is clear and deep ocean-blue, the iris on his right one is much paler and foggy. There's some heavy scarring on the skin around it, and on the eyelid, as if someone tried to remove his eye.

"I have around 5 percent sight left in my right eye," he says in a detached voice, "but it interferes with the sight in my left one, making everything blurry. I wear the patch all the time, except when sleeping, working out, or showering."

Oh, Mikhail . . .what happened to you? I wonder if he'll ever tell me. With me sitting this high up, we're almost face to face, so I lean forward until our noses touch and put my palms on either side of his face, feeling the harsh ridges marring his skin.

"Jesus, Bianca." He closes his eyes and touches his forehead to mine. "How can you bear to look at me?"

I reach out with my hand to remove a strand of his hair that's has fallen over his forehead and brush the back of my palm down his right cheek. The pain he experienced sustaining this must have been unbearable. The longest of the scars is breaking his right eyebrow into two parts, and I trace my finger along it, then down his nose, until I reach his mouth.

"I think . . ." My throat screams in pain, as the cracked whisper leaves my lips, but I continue anyway. "You are . . . hot."

I cup his face with my palms and place a kiss on his lips. Then another one. I am obsessed with his lips.

"You are crazy, solnyshko."

Nope, not crazy. Just in love with him.

I don't care about the scars or his eye. To me, he's the most handsome man I've ever met. Slowly, I glide my hands down his chest and abs until I reach the waistband of his pants and start unbuttoning them. Mikhail lets out a sound resembling a growl, grabs me around the waist, and carries me toward his bedroom.

"Clothes off," he says as he deposits me on the bed.

I scramble out of my T-shirt and jeans in record time, and fumble with the clasp on my bra while he hooks his fingers on the waistband of my panties and slides them down my legs.

"You are"—he places a kiss on my ankle—"so fucking beautiful." Another kiss, this one on the inside of my thigh.

I watch him as he bends down, buries his face between my legs, and licks my pussy.

"I'm not much to look at,"—another lick—"but I'll make sure you never think about any other man, Bianca."

He thrusts one finger inside me and starts sucking my clit. It's too much, but at the same time, I want more. He adds another finger, and oh God, I think I'm going to combust. His fingers are straining my walls, his tongue circling my clit, and I arch my back from the bed as a wave of pleasure rocks my body. Mikhail removes his mouth from my pussy, and suddenly, I feel the tip of his cock at my entrance, but he doesn't thrust inside me right away. Instead, his big body looms over mine, his hand clutching the back of my neck as he looks down on me with mismatched eyes.

"Mine!" He growls as he starts sliding his cock inside me so slowly, I feel as if I'm going to lose my mind. "If I see any man touch you, I'm going to kill him, Bianca." He places his palm on my cheek and thrusts himself inside me, then retreats.

I take a sharp breath and my eyes roll back into my head. Mikhail lifts my legs and rests them on his shoulders allowing him to get deeper inside of me. He hits *that* spot again, and I can feel myself getting closer to climax. When he forces my hips up off the bed and drives into me, tremors start rocking my body. White stars explode behind my eyelids as I ride out my orgasm, while Mikhail continues to pound into me, destroying me in the best way possible.

Chapter eleven

Mikhail

Happiness. I don't remember the last time I felt truly happy. Satisfied, yes. But this thrill, this feeling of weightlessness filling my whole body, is completely foreign. I look down at Bianca who's snuggled into my side, her hand on my chest, and one leg tucked between mine, and my heart warms.

"I have to get up," I whisper and place a kiss at the top of Bianca's head. "Sisi will be here with Lena in half an hour."

She looks up at me, smiles, and reaches for my hand to inspect my fingers. Satisfied the Band-Aids are still in place, she sits up and motions for me to turn around. The window shades are rolled up and the whole room is bathed in light, putting every mark on my skin on full display. Still, I turn onto my stomach, and looking at the window, I wait.

She places her palm on my lower back and slowly moves her hand upward, her touch impossibly light. I feel a tingling sensation when her hair falls onto my skin, and then her lips, placing a kiss between my shoulder blades where the scarring is the worst.

"Please . . . don't do that."

The tingling sensation travels upward as the tips of her hair tease the skin just below my shoulder, and she bends and whispers in my ear, "Why?"

"Jesus, baby, how can you even ask?"

"I like . . . you, Mikhail," she says, her voice barely audible. "Every . . . single . . . part . . . of you."

The last word gets lost, and the only thing I hear are her short breaths as the chill runs down my spine. I spring up to a sitting position, cradle her face in my palms, and hope I'm wrong. "It hurts when you speak, doesn't it?"

She looks at me, and nods.

I close my eyes and kiss her forehead. I should be put down like the asshole I am. A selfish, lying asshole who made her hurt herself for no reason.

"You will never do that again." I put my finger on her lips. "Promise me."

Her face falls, but she nods again, making me feel even worse. Fuck. I get up from the bed, put my pants on, and stand in front of the window, looking at the people hurrying about on the sidewalk below. She'll hate me.

I put my hands at the back of my head and take a deep breath. "I need to tell you something."

Mikhail is acting strange all of a sudden, pacing back and forth in front of the window. He stops for a second, looks at me, then shakes his head and resumes pacing. Did something happen? It must be something bad, because I don't remember ever seeing him so distraught.

Finally, he stops and turns toward me. "I know you'll be mad, and you have every right to be. I hope you'll forgive me for not telling you right away. I'm sorry."

My eyes go wide, my jaw nearly hitting the floor as I watch his fingers making familiar shapes while he talks. The way his hands move, quickly and with ease . . . my God, he's not just familiar with sign language. I know just enough for an everyday conversation. I would never be able to have philosophical discussions and such. But the way Mikhail signs, it's evident he's a pro.

"*Why?*" I sign and stare at him, making sure all the sadness and disappointment are visible on my face.

"Because it would have required explaining, and I wasn't ready to give that to you. I'm sorry."

"*And you couldn't just say so?*"

I get off the bed and, without looking at him, go straight to the guest room, slamming the door with all my might.

The sound of Lena's giggling reaches my ears, and I sit up in the bed. I spent two hours lying there, looking at the ceiling, thinking.

Mikhail knows sign language, and he didn't say a word about it this whole time. It was selfish and rude, like putting earplugs in your ears on purpose, just so you won't hear what the other person has to say. I feel so betrayed.

"But I want pancakes," Lena's voice reaches me through the door. "Please, Daddy."

I don't hear what Mikhail says, only Lena's unhappy reply. "Okay, Daddy."

When I exit the guest room, I see Mikhail standing by the counter, a pan and a carton of eggs in front of him. Lena is sitting on the floor in the living room, playing with the book we bought the other day, but when she sees me coming, she jumps up and runs in my direction.

"Bianca, can you make pancakes? Daddy doesn't know how to make pancakes. Can you make pancakes?"

I smile, brush the back of my palm over her rosy cheek, and nod.

She squeals in delight, grabs my hand, and starts dragging me toward the kitchen. "Daddy, Daddy, Bianca will make pancakes."

She ushers me over to the stove, and I find myself standing next to Mikhail, with my shoulder brushing his arm. Lena lets go of my hand and runs back to the living room, leaving me alone with my deceiver of a husband.

"You don't have to," he says without looking at me. "I'll make her scrambled eggs."

I ignore him and go to the other side of the kitchen to get the mixer from the drawer, then open the cupboard to take out a bowl. It's on the second shelf, so I raise onto my toes and reach for it. Two large hands circle my waist as Mikhail lifts me the last couple of inches. Once I get what I'm after, he lowers me down without a word, then leaves the kitchen and heads to sit on the floor next to Lena. She takes the book and moves onto his lap, and I watch him as he points at something on the page and starts making animal noises. Lena giggles and kisses him on the cheek, then points to something else.

I start making the pancake batter but can't resist throwing a look at them every few minutes. He is so strange, my husband. I don't understand him, and I'm still mad at him, but I can't make myself ignore his presence. It's as if a magical force is pulling me toward him. Even though I'm mad, it takes a great deal of self-control to keep myself from going over there just to be closer to him.

While I am waiting for the pancakes to cook, I scroll through my messages on my phone. There are three from Milene, asking how things are and asking about Nonna's present. Shit. I forgot about it again. I send her a quick text saying everything is fine and asking about school. The next message is from Angelo.

> **11:17 Angelo:** Everybody knows Mikhail fucking Orlov! I can't believe Dad went through with it! Are you okay? I don't know when I'll be back. I have some shit to deal with here, but as soon as I'm back I'm coming to see you. If he does something to you, you need to tell me right away and I'll handle him.

I flip the pancakes and read the message one more time, confused. What does he think Mikhail is doing to me?

> **21:13 Bianca:** I'm great. What's the problem with me being married to Mikhail? Did you two get in a fight at some point or something?

My mom's message is next. She's asking again about the shopping trip I promised. I ignore it, put my phone away and go back to the pancakes.

I'm almost done when Mikhail's phone rings. He takes the call, and for a few moments, he just listens to the person on the other end, then curses. Scooping Lena up, he carries her into the kitchen, places her on one of the barstools, and turns toward me.

"Can you watch Lena for an hour or so? Something came up and it's too late to call Sisi."

I nod and pour more batter into the pan.

"I won't be long."

There's a light kiss at the top of my head, and then he's gone. I close my eyes and take a deep breath. It's hard to stay mad at Mikhail when every cell of my body seems, somehow, attuned to him, yearning to get closer.

It's well into the night when I park my car inside the warehouse. I jump out and head toward the corner where the Albanian guy from this morning is sitting on the floor. He looks half dead. I turn to Denis, who's standing next to him, and grit my teeth.

"Where the fuck is the doc?" I bite out.

"He's out of the city. Can't get here before tomorrow. I told him the guy's symptoms, and he said it's either a serious concussion, or he has intracranial bleeding. He needs to go to a hospital."

I look down at the asshole sitting in a puddle of his vomit. "He dared to shoot at the car while my wife was inside. He's not going anywhere."

There's a bottle of water on a nearby chair, so I grab it and splash the contents over the guy's head. He shudders, mumbles something incoherent, and leans back onto the wall. Based on how pale he is, and the unfocused look in his eyes, he won't last long. I'll have to work fast.

I walk back to my car, open the trunk, and take out a toolbox. On the outside, it looks like an ordinary toolkit, but removing the interior box reveals a hidden compartment, where I keep the real tools of my trade. I grab one of the syringes and a scalpel, and head back.

"What's that?" Denis asks, pointing to the syringe.

"Adrenaline shot," I say as I bury the needle into the side of the guy's neck. "It might make him more coherent for a little bit. I've never tried it on someone with a concussion."

"So, it will make him better? Why didn't Doc think of that?"

"Because Doc doesn't kill people for a living." I throw the syringe to the side, crouch, and take the Albanian's hand. "When the adrenaline leaves his system, he'll crash. Hard. Grab his shoulders and keep him still."

Holding the guy by his wrist, I force his palm to the floor and place the scalpel at the root of his thumb. The Albanian becomes coherent at the exact moment I cut his finger off and starts screaming.

"Shut the fuck up!" I slap him across his face. Not the wisest thing to do considering his condition, but I'm in a bad mood. "Listen to me carefully. You are going to die tonight. It can be quick, or I can make sure it's extremely painful and long-lasting. Nod if you understand."

He whimpers and nods, trying to pull out his hand from my grip. I swipe the scalpel and cut off another of his fingers, which results in another screaming fit.

"Who sent you to intercept us, and what were your orders?" I yell into his face.

"I don't know," he chokes out. "Arben talked with the guy who paid for the job."

"Who's Arben?"

He mumbles something and closes his eyes. It looks like the adrenaline isn't working.

I slap him again. "I said, who is Arben?"

"The driver."

One of the guys I shot. Fuck! "What did they want you to do?"

"Kill the man with the eye patch." He looks up at me and shudders. "It was just a job."

"What about the woman?"

"The guy said she's not important."

Not important. I take a deep breath, trying to keep myself from killing him right away. "Anything else?"

"N-n-no."

"Do you know what the man who met with Arben looked like?"

"No." His voice is barely audible now.

Fuck. I stand up and take the gun from the holster under my jacket. "Not important," I spit out and shoot him in the head.

Turning toward Denis, I pin him with my gaze. "Make sure you're not late next time, Denis."

He takes a step back. "Of course, Boss."

"Good. Clean up this mess."

It's almost four in the morning and I'm starting to worry. Where's Mikhail?

When Lena fell asleep, I went to the kitchen to tidy up the mess, and then took a quick shower, expecting him to be back by the time I finished. Has something happened?

I take one of the T-shirts I stole from him and put it on. I'm finishing braiding my hair when I feel rough palms covering my hands. I release the strands, and my hair falls as I look up at Mikhail's reflection in the mirror. He stands behind me and divides my hair into three sections again, then starts braiding my hair for me. His moves might be a little clumsy, but it looks like he knows what he's doing.

"My sister always pestered me to braid her hair when our mother wasn't around," he says without meeting my eyes, and there's so much pain in that one sentence, it pierces me right through my heart.

"Oksana was deaf from birth. She was four years older than me, so I learned sign language before I learned to read."

It's not just the fact he's using the past tense. I can feel it in the tone of his voice . . . Something bad happened to his sister. Mikhail raises his head and our gazes collide in the mirror. There is such a haunted look in his eye, and I know for certain whatever happened is much worse than I can imagine.

I take the hair tie from the dresser, offer it to Mikhail, and wait for him to secure the braid.

"Not my best work, I'm afraid." He sighs. "You might want to do it again."

"*It's perfect,*" I sign into the mirror.

Mikhail places his hands on my hips, turns me around, and raises his hand to run a finger down the side of my face. "I'm sorry."

I sigh, pull on his arm until he bends, and I place a kiss on his lips.

"Am I forgiven?"

"*Not yet. You will need to work much more for that.*"

He raises his left eyebrow, and his lips widen slightly. "What did you have in mind? Some kind of manual labor?"

"*Yes.*" I smile and start unbuttoning his shirt.

I feel his hands on my stomach, slowly pulling on my shirt. "I better start then."

He pulls the shirt over my head, removes my panties, and turns me to face the mirror, with my bare back pressed to his chest. I stare at our reflections—me completely naked, and him standing behind me in his black shirt and dress pants. He places a kiss on my neck while his hands come to my waist and slowly start sliding down, over my hip bones and then lower.

"I want you to watch"—his right hand slides even lower, between my legs—"how beautiful you are when you come."

His palm glides against my pussy as he bites my shoulder at the same time, making me shudder from the combined sensation. One finger enters my core, and I grab onto his forearm, pressing myself onto his hand. There's something improper about seeing myself like this, with him touching me so intimately while he's still fully clothed.

His other hand slides down, his finger circling my clit, then presses the spot at the top of my pussy. A silent moan escapes my lips and I close my eyes, enjoying the sensation.

"Eyes on the mirror, Bianca. Or I stop."

I open my eyes instantly.

"Good girl."

I can't remove my eyes from our reflection in the mirror. Mikhail's huge body pressed up against mine, his hands between my legs, his lips trailing a line of kisses on my shoulder. Another finger enters me as he starts teasing my clit with his other hand, changing the tempo from slow to fast, then slow again, making my body tremble harder.

"Come for me, my little lamb," he whispers in my ear and curls his fingers inside me while pressing onto my clit, and I explode.

The tremors rocking my body are so strong I can't hold myself upright, so I grasp his forearm with both of my hands and watch Mikhail in the mirror. Composed. Not a hair out of place. Looking straight into my eyes. Wicked, wicked man. The silent types are always the most dangerous.

Chapter Twelve

Mikhail

SHE HAS BEEN STEALING MY CLOTHES. BY MY CURRENT calculation, she has taken at least four T-shirts, my favorite hoodie, and one dress shirt, so far. And it looks like she's decided she needs another hoodie for her collection.

"Will this one do?" I ask.

"*Yes. Perfect.*" Bianca takes the black hoodie I'm holding, puts it on, and starts rolling up the sleeves.

I know she got the rest of her things. Denis went to her father's place two days ago and brought back the boxes her sister packed.

"Any chance I'll get that one back?" I say and caress her face with the back of my hand.

She looks up at me, smirks, and shakes her head. My little thief. I smile, take her chin to tilt her head, and kiss her.

"Sisi, Sisi, they are kissing again!" Lena shouts from somewhere behind me. "Roby asked to kiss me today and I said okay. He kissed me on the cheek. I'll tell him to kiss me on my mouth tomorrow."

My head snaps up. I turn on my heel, stride toward the kitchen where Lena is watching Sisi prepare lunch, and crouch in front of my daughter.

"No kissing boys, Lena. You're too young for that."

"I am not. I am going to marry Roby," she says seriously, and Sisi bursts out laughing.

Jesus. I didn't expect to have this conversation for another decade. "Why do you want to marry Roby? Is he a nice person?"

"No, he always fights with other boys."

"Then why do you want to marry him, zayka?"

"He has two dogs and a parakeet, Daddy!"

"Would you like to have a pet, Lenochka? A goldfish maybe?" Please, just don't say a parakeet.

"I want a parakeet, Daddy! Please, please can I have a parakeet? Sisi, Bianca, Daddy said I can have a parakeet! Can we go buy a parakeet now? Daddy, when are we going to buy my parakeet?"

Wonderful. I sigh. "Okay. We'll go buy a parakeet next week, Lena."

"Yes!" she squeals in delight and starts running around the dining room table.

There's a light touch on my right forearm. I turn my head and find Bianca standing there, watching me with an amused expression on her face.

"Do you think she'll stop talking about marrying Roby when she gets the parakeet?" I ask.

"No," Bianca mouths and smiles.

"Yeah, I don't think so, either."

"*You are a remarkable father,*" she signs. "*She is lucky to have you.*"

I place my palm on her cheek. She has no idea how much her words mean to me.

"Mikhail," Sisi says from the kitchen, "there's a parent-teacher meeting scheduled for tomorrow afternoon at day care. Do you want me to go?"

"Daddy will go to the meeting!" Lena shouts from under the table. "Daddy, will you go?"

"Daddy will go to the meeting, zayka."

"Can Bianca come? Bianca, will you come with Daddy?"

I look down at Bianca to find her watching me. "You don't have to go."

"*I would love to come,*" she signs, cocks her head to the side, then continues. "*You don't like going to Lena's day care?*"

I touch her chin. I didn't think I was so easy to read. "No."

"*Why?*"

"Because some of Lena's friends are scared of me."

She rolls her eyes. "*Children can be stupid sometimes.*"

My little lamb. Most days, she seems much more mature than her twenty-one years, but the truth is, she's too innocent. If she wasn't, she would probably see what those kids unconsciously feel—that they should turn around and run as fast as they can the moment they see me coming.

Chapter Thirteen

Mikhail

Bianca wanted to shop for a present for her grandmother, and I expected us to go to a mall or a jewelry store. Instead, I find myself in a small, cramped shop that specializes in custom-made hats. When we enter, I become convinced she's given me the wrong address. None of the things displayed here looks like a hat. Everything is multicolored feathers and ikebana. One, in particular, attracts my attention and looks like a dead bird.

Bianca points to something resembling a blue plate with an assortment of white and green artificial flowers springing from it. It's atrocious.

"Are you serious?"

She just nods, takes the blue-green monstrosity, and puts it on her head. I find it hard not to laugh when she walks to the mirror and starts turning her head left and right, regarding the hat from every angle. Even with the crazy thing on, my wife is heart-stoppingly beautiful. She's wearing a flowery skirt that reaches her knees, and has paired it with a beige top and heels in the same color. I've grown used to seeing her with her hair loose or in a braid, but today, she's twisted it into a bun at the top of her head. I think she wants to make a good impression with the day care teacher. She turns to me and signs, *"We are taking it."* Then, she carries the awful hat to the checkout.

When we leave the shop, I take Bianca's hand and lead her toward the small restaurant with outdoor tables I noticed a little further down the sidewalk. I have to go to work after we pick up Lena, and I won't be back until late, so I want to spend a bit more time with her.

We take one of the side tables, and while we're waiting for the food, I survey our surroundings. This situation with the Albanians is starting to worry me.

"So, you're sure your grandmother will like that . . . thing?" I sip my wine and look at the box laying on the corner of the table.

"She'll love it," Bianca signs and digs into her food.

I highly doubt it. "She has strange taste then."

"Everybody thinks Nonna Giulia is a little bit crazy."

"You don't?"

"No. She just pretends she is, so she can get away with anything. She hired male strippers for her last birthday."

Bianca bursts out laughing when I almost choke on my wine. I love her smile, the way it reaches her eyes reminds me of a sunray on a dark stormy day.

"V tvoyikh glazakh kusochek neba, solnyshko."

She looks at me, confused, so I translate for her. "It means, 'there is a piece of the sky in your eyes.'"

I find it hard to believe, but her cheeks actually turn a little red. Sometimes I forget how young she is.

"Does the age difference between us bother you?" I ask.

All things considered, I assume the ten-year age difference is the least problematic thing.

"No. Why?"

"I don't know. Maybe you'd like to go out every night, party, do what other . . . girls your age do."

"Most of the girls my age haven't been training six hours a day since they were twelve. Partying until morning was never my thing. But I wouldn't object if my husband took me dancing sometimes. Or are you too old for that?"

I lean over the table, take her chin between my fingers, and kiss her pouty lips. "We'll see."

"How is work?"

"Same as always. Pakhan's wife invited us for dinner on Monday. Do you want to go?"

"Sure. How is she? She wasn't at the wedding."

"Three months pregnant, and very unpleasant lately. I think she might end up killing Roman."

"Why?"

"Let's just say Roman's behavior became a bit extreme once he found out she's pregnant. You'll see."

"You never told me what you do for the Bratva."

"I organize drug distribution," I say.

"Do you know my brother? Angelo?"

An interesting question. "I don't think we've met."

"Strange. I got the impression he knows you."

Yes, he probably knows of me. Most of the people in our circles do. I need to change the direction of this conversation.

"When did you start with ballet?"

"My mom took me to my first lesson when I was four. I started with more intensive training at six."

"Fifteen years. Must have been hard to leave all that behind."

"The hardest thing I've ever done. I could have stayed, taken some side roles with less demanding choreography. Fewer jumps. Instead, I decided to retire. To leave while I was still at the top. It's vain, I know."

"It's not vain." I take her hand and brush my thumb over the inside of her palm. So soft. "What happened to your voice, Bianca?"

I feel her go still. She pulls her hand from mine, takes a sip of her orange juice, and looks somewhere behind me.

"I was eleven. Father was driving me to training. It was Sunday, around seven in the morning. There was a party the previous night, they were celebrating something. He was still slightly drunk. We crashed."

I watch as she takes a deep breath and looks at me.

"They said I wasn't breathing when the ambulance came. They had to intubate me on the spot. The paramedic who did it was young and scared. He messed up something. Damaged my vocal cords."

"And your father?"

"Dislocated shoulder." She smiles and looks away. *"Bruno Scardoni is like a cockroach."*

It's evident she doesn't want to talk about it anymore.

"I'm sorry." I reach for her hand and kiss the tops of her fingers.

Someone needs to kill that asshole.

I don't like the way Lena's teacher is looking at Mikhail. From the moment we entered the playroom, she's been throwing looks in our direction every now and then, so I move closer to him and wrap my arm around his waist. The teacher talks about books she recommends parents buy for next month's activities, and, for a moment, her eyes wander to me, looking me over from head to toe as if she's sizing me up. It's evident she's taken a liking to Mikhail, and I don't like it one bit.

After she's finished listing the materials, some of the parents gather to discuss their child's progress, but Mikhail and I stay in the back and wait until the crowd dissipates. As we approach the teacher, I let my arm fall away from Mikhail's waist, and decide to stay a few steps back. It doesn't feel right to butt in.

"Mr. Orlov," the teacher says in a sugary voice. "We haven't seen you for quite some time."

She's pretty, looks to be in her early thirties, and based on the huge grin on her face, she *really* likes my husband.

"How's Lena doing? Any problems?" Mikhail asks, ignoring her comment.

"Oh, Lena is a wonderful child, so well-behaved. You are doing such a great job with her." She bats her lashes at him like a lovesick schoolgirl, and my vision goes red. I cover the few feet separating us in two seconds, wrap my hand around Mikhail's waist again, and smile.

Mikhail's arm comes around my back. "Miss Lewis," he says, "This is Bianca. My wife."

I can't remember the last time I felt as much satisfaction as I do now, watching her eyes go as wide as saucers. That's right, bitch. He's taken. As you should have already deduced yourself.

"If that's all, we should go. Lena is waiting for us in the hallway." Mikhail nods toward the door.

"Yes, of course."

As we're leaving, I throw a look over my shoulder to find the teacher watching us. Without moving my eyes from hers, I slide my hand from Mikhail's lower back down until it lands on his rock-hard ass, and I can't resist squeezing just a little.

When we exit into the hallway, Mikhail bends to whisper in my ear. "Did you just squeeze my ass?"

"Maybe," I mouth and do it again.

"Daddy, Daddy!" Lena hops up from the little bench on our right and jumps into Mikhail's arms. "Can we go buy my parakeet now, Daddy?"

Mikhail sighs and kisses her forehead. "Yes."

We drop by the pet store on the way home, and Lena chooses a little blue parakeet. While Mikhail asks the store attendant for the guidelines on feeding, Lena and I go to the rack on the left to pick up some bird toys. The door to the store opens and two boys Lena's age rush inside, followed by their mother, and run toward the fish tanks displayed on the wall.

"Mommy, I want a goldfish!" one of the boys yells.

"I don't want a goldfish. I want a black one, like Batman!" the other exclaims. "Goldfish are for girls."

They're still fighting over the fish when we leave the store, and as we walk toward the car, I look down at Lena, who has suddenly gone unusually quiet. I expected her to be excited, but she doesn't say a word while Mikhail places the cage with the bird in the backseat, and straps Lena into her car seat. It's strange, she usually babbles nonstop.

When we're all inside and Mikhail reaches to start the car, Lena finally speaks. "Daddy? Where is my mommy?"

Mikhail's hand stills with the keys midway to the ignition.

He takes a deep breath, then turns and takes her small hand in his. "Your mommy is with the angels now, zayka."

"Why?"

"She . . . she was sick, Lenochka."

"Like Charley's daddy?"

"Yes, zayka. Like Charley's daddy."

I reach over and place my hand on Mikhail's thigh. This is hard for him. I see it in the way he's squeezing the wheel with his other hand, his knuckles white from the strain.

Lena cocks her head to the side, looks at me for a moment, and turns to Mikhail. "Charley has a new daddy now. Is Bianca my new mommy?"

My breath catches, and at the same time, I feel Mikhail's body going stone-still under my hand. We've never talked about what Lena should call me. I'd assumed it would be Bianca but haven't counted on the fact she's too young to understand. Based on the slightly panicked expression on Mikhail's face, he wasn't expecting this either. We should have, though.

"You remember when we talked about this? That Daddy and Bianca were getting married, and we'd all be living together?"

"Yes, Daddy. Charley's new daddy is also living with them."

We should have assumed "Daddy's wife" might equal "Mommy" for her. I've always wanted children, but it seemed like something that wouldn't happen soon. I don't think I'd mind if Lena starts to call me mom. I consider it for a moment. No, I wouldn't mind at all. In fact, I like the idea. If Mikhail is okay with it, of course.

"Well, Lenochka, it's . . ." Mikhail starts, but I squeeze his thigh and he turns to me.

"You can say yes. If it's all right with you."

He doesn't say anything, just stares at me. Maybe he doesn't like the idea of Lena considering me as her new mom. The realization hurts, but I make sure it doesn't show on my face.

"You don't have to. I just . . ." I sigh. *"It's okay. We can try explaining it to her."*

Mikhail reaches out with his hand, cups my cheek, and leans forward. "Lena never talked about her mother, and"—he closes his eye and curses—"I fucked up. I thought she understood. She's too young. I should have tried to explain things better. You and I should've talked first. I can't ask this of you, Bianca."

"You are a good father, and you didn't fuck up anything." I sign and brush his hand. *"And I'm okay with Lena thinking of me as her new mom."*

"You're twenty-one, baby." Mikhail furrows his brows.

"My mother had Angelo when she was nineteen. It's okay."

"Are you sure?"

I lean in and place my lips over his. "Yes," I whisper into his mouth and kiss him.

Chapter fourteen

Mikhail

I'M LEANING ON THE COUNTER IN THE KITCHEN AND scrolling through my phone for updates on work when Bianca walks in. I look up and my breathing stops for a moment. Wearing a long black dress that wraps around her upper body and then falls to the ground in numerous layers of silky fabric, and with her hair in a thick braid, she looks like she stepped off the pages of a fashion magazine. She sees me looking, smiles, and turns around twice, making the silky fabric float around her, revealing her black stilettos and slender legs through a deep slit on the side. I can't take my eyes off her.

"What do you think?" she signs.

I'm not capable of rational thought, and the only thing currently on my mind is her, naked, in my bed.

"Ty zazhgla ogon' v moyey dushe, solnyshko."

She smirks, approaches me, and starts tracing the shape of a question mark on my chest with her finger.

"It means, 'you've ignited a fire in my soul, Bianca.' And if we don't leave immediately, we won't be going at all."

Her lips widen in a smile, and she takes my hand and leads me toward the door. She keeps smiling in the car as we leave the garage, and I'm wondering what could be on her mind when she leans in and whispers in my ear.

"I don't . . . have panties."

The car swerves, but I manage to righten it, barely avoiding the concrete pillar on the side. When I have it under control, I turn toward Bianca to find her leaning back in her seat, wearing a self-satisfied smirk on her face.

There are four large tents set up on the expansive manicured lawn. At least two hundred guests are milling around long tables covered in white cloth, chatting with each other, and laughing at what are probably lame jokes. Most of them are Italians. Some of them I remember seeing at our wedding reception. There are also a few politicians. An interesting lot for sure.

In the middle of the largest group stands a small frail woman, wearing a poison-green dress and a strange spiky thing on top of her head of gray hair. An extremely attractive and young man—probably in his midtwenties—has his arm wrapped around her waist and is whispering something into the woman's ear.

Bianca squeezes my hand, and I look down at her to find her smiling widely, motioning with her head toward the woman in a green dress. I guess she's the famous Nonna Giulia.

We approach the group, and I take note of each person who enters my field of vision, cataloging anything even remotely suspicious. I don't like crowds, but I'm not a fan of wide-open spaces either. Both are a security risk.

Bianca's grandmother turns, and the moment she notices us, she giggles in delight like a little girl, then hurries over to us. Her young companion trails after her.

"Bianca! You're late!" She kisses Bianca on both cheeks, then turns to me. "I see you brought your husband. Handsome. Tall. Fit." She leans in slightly, regarding me. "You picked good, *tesoro*."

Not only crazy but blind as well, apparently. I nod. "I'm glad you approve, Mrs. Mancini."

"Oh God, no. Just call me Nonna. Mrs. Mancini sounds like an old woman's name. And I was divorced two months ago, anyway," she says and makes a shooing motion to the young man standing next to her. "Go get something to eat, Tony. I'll find you later."

The guy nods and leaves without question.

"I hired him specifically for today. The young ones are expensive, but it'll be so worth it. Bruno is going to lose his mind." She smiles widely, and I'm not sure if she's not a little bit nuts.

Bianca takes out her phone, types, and gives it to Giulia, who looks at the screen, then up at Bianca.

"Of course. Why, do you have something against gigolos? It's honest work. Oh, there's Luca Rossi. It's too bad he's already married. Such a fine male specimen." She narrows her eyes. "Is that Franco with him? I hear he divorced his wife last month, so it's open season. I have to go."

I look down at Bianca, who's shaking her head as she watches her grandmother rushing toward the man, presumably Franco.

"She is just fooling around." Bianca signs. *"Let's go find somewhere to sit."*

We choose one of the miraculously free tables on the side and watch the crowd in silence. The waiter brings our drinks, and Bianca reaches for my glass, moving it from my right side to the left. I don't think she did it consciously, as she looks too focused on picking out a canapé from the plate in front of us. She must have noticed I don't keep drinks on my blind side. Strange how she doesn't seem to care her husband only has one eye. I know very well what a mess my right eye is, so I still expect her to recoil when she wakes up in my arms and looks up at me. But she just smiles and goes back to sleep for a few more minutes. My Bianca is not a morning person.

There are a lot of men around, and my wife looks especially desirable in her dress today. And with nothing underneath.

I grab her chair and pull it closer to me. "Baby," I bend to whisper in her ear, "come sit on my lap."

I look up at Mikhail, raise an eyebrow, then get up and stand between his legs. He taps his left thigh and looks at me pointedly, as if he is daring me. Mikhail never does anything without a reason, and I'm curious what he has in mind, so I turn and sit on his leg.

"Quite a crowd. Your nonna is popular," he says.

His hand finds the slit of my dress, and the next second, there is a touch of a finger on my knee, before it slowly travels higher over the inner side of my thigh. It lingers there for a moment, then starts going up. He's crazy. I blink and turn my head to look at him.

"Something wrong?" he asks, his face the embodiment of calm and innocence, as if he doesn't have his hand buried between my legs.

I take the side of my dress, place the length of fabric over his hand and forearm, and look back toward the mass of guests. Two can play this game.

"I wonder," he says quietly as his finger reaches my naked core and presses onto my clit. "Will they find our sitting arrangement proper?"

I take a deep breath and open my legs slightly, thankful for the table hiding us from view.

"You know, I've noted at least twenty men undressing you with their eyes since we got here," he whispers, and suddenly, his finger enters me. "I don't like that, Bianca."

As his finger deftly plays with my pussy, my breathing gets faster, and it becomes harder to keep my face expressionless. I can't believe I'm sitting in front of two hundred people with Mikhail's finger inside me. Or how damn good it makes me feel. Oh God, a waiter with a tray full of desserts is coming in our direction. I grab Mikhail's forearm and start tugging at his arm, but he ignores me completely and teases my clit with his thumb.

"I am a very jealous man." His finger curls, causing me to bite my lip to suppress a moan. "I don't deal well with other men ogling my wife."

The pressure building between my legs skyrockets.

"No one is allowed to look at you, Bianca. Just me." He pinches my clit, buries a second finger inside of me, then moves it deftly in a stroking motion against my walls. The waiter is getting closer, but instead of stopping, Mikhail picks up the pace. Just when I think I'm going to lose it, he presses firmly onto my clit and I come all over his hand.

I am still feeling the aftershocks when the waiter arrives at our table.

"No, thank you," Mikhail says nonchalantly and looks at me. "Do you want something?"

I quickly shake my head. The moment the waiter turns his back to us, I grab my wine glass and empty it. I can't believe he did that. Here.

"We should go to parties more often," Mikhail says and takes a napkin from the table. Reaching under my dress, he starts cleaning me up.

"*You are insane,*" I sign.

Mikhail only shrugs and nods toward the entrance. "Your family is here."

I watch the group entering the grounds. Her father is first, with Bianca's mother on his arm. They're both impeccably dressed, and the only thing standing out is a bandage around his right hand. The letter opener obviously did significant damage since it's been three weeks. When Bruno notices us, his steps falter for a second, and he sends me a look that could scorch the grass under my feet. I lift my glass in his direction, enjoying the angry look spreading over his face. Bianca's older sister, Allegra, follows behind her parents with her spine ramrod straight, and her head held high like she owns the place. Milene is last, walking hand in hand with another girl her age. They're laughing, whispering, and ogling Tony, who's leaning on one of the pillars next to the dance floor.

"Your baby sister is ogling your granny's date," I comment.

Bianca's eyes go wide, and she jumps up from my lap, grabbing my forearm.

"I'll wait here. It wouldn't be wise for me to go near your father." I run my hand down her arm and lace our fingers together, then look up into her whiskey-colored eyes. It's still puzzling me, how much I enjoy touching her. "I may decide he doesn't need his other hand, either."

She huffs and scrunches her nose. *"I'll be right back."*

I watch Bianca hurry toward her sister, signing with her hands even before she reaches Milene. Her moves are sharp and agitated. She's so cute when she's mad.

"She's really something, isn't she?" Nonna Giulia says as she takes a seat in Bianca's chair next to me.

"Yes."

Milene is whispering something, and I see Bianca slap herself over the forehead, then she signs to her sister, looking very annoyed. Looks like Milene wants to hire Tony for her birthday, as well.

"You two are a strange pairing, my boy," Giulia says. "I always expected her to end up with one of the dancers from her company, or maybe an artist. Someone . . . easygoing. I thought she would need someone less . . . hard."

I don't comment, because I'm sure she's not wrong.

"I married six times, you know?" she continues. "Everyone thinks I'm a little bit wacky in the head . . . the crazy Giulia who changes her husbands like they're socks.

But I was just trying to find a man who would look at me the way Vitallo, my first husband, looked at me."

"And how would that be?" I ask.

"The way you look at my Bianca. Like you would lay your body over a field of burning coals, so she could cross it without burning her feet."

I appraise the woman silently. Nonna is not as crazy as people think, and much more attentive than I gave her credit for.

"Bianca is different around you, you know," she continues. "There were only two boyfriends before you. She was never really into dating, even when she was Milene's age. But boys were always drawn to her. Allegra hated her for it."

"She's her sister, how can she hate her?"

"Never underestimate the power of a woman's vanity. It got worse after Marcus. Oh, Allegra really lost it. She had her eyes on him for years. He was a good catch, the son of the real estate mogul. But Marcus only had eyes for Bianca. He and Bianca got together, and not even a month later he told Bruno he wanted to marry her."

Deep anger starts building inside of me just with the barest idea of Bianca being married to someone else.

"Bianca said no and broke up with him." Giulia shrugs. "I didn't understand it then, they seemed like a nice couple. But I understand now."

I turn toward her and cock my head. "What, exactly?"

Nonna sighs and shakes her head. "He still has one eye left, but he's blind as a bat anyway."

I see Bianca signing something to Milene. When she kisses her sister and turns to walk in our direction, a man approaches her and starts telling her something. He's in his late twenties, blond, and based on the way he's speaking to her, they know each other very well.

"Speak of the devil." Giulia tsks next to me. "Marcus Kuch himself. He never really got over Bianca rejecting him and . . ."

I don't hear the rest, because the moment I see the asshole put his hand on Bianca's upper arm, I spring to my feet and head toward him while a murderous rage starts consuming me.

I manage to convince Milene she cannot hire Nonna's gigolo for her next birthday and head back to our table when Marcus appears in front of me. We didn't break up on the best of terms, but I have nothing personally against him, so I stop for a moment, intending to be polite.

"Is that him? Is that the monster they married you off to?" He gets in my face. "Is it true he bought you from your father, like people are saying?"

I am so shocked by his words, I can only stare at him.

"Allegra told me he's keeping you like some prisoner in his home."

What the hell? I'm going to kill her.

"Is it true he's beating you, Bianca?"

I can't listen to this crap anymore, so I turn to leave only to see my husband coming toward us with murder written all over his face.

Mikhail passes me, wraps his hand around Marcus's neck,

and yanks him close enough that they're nose-to-nose. "How dare you touch my wife!" he sneers through his teeth.

I groan inwardly and duck under Mikhail's arm to insert myself between them, placing my palms on my husband's chest and shaking my head. Mikhail looks at me, then at Marcus, and starts squeezing his neck. He's going to strangle him. I try pulling on Mikhail's arm, but he tightens his grip while Marcus tries to pry his fingers away and fights for breath. Everyone stares. Fuck. Fuck. Fuck! I raise onto the tips of my toes and hook my hands around Mikhail's neck.

"Mikhail," I say, hoping that hearing my voice will shake him from his anger. "Please."

He looks down at me and holds my gaze for a few seconds, then looks back at Marcus. "If I see you near my wife again," he barks and lets go, "you're dead."

As expected, Marcus turns on his heel and runs off, coughing. He was always a coward. I'm so angry at him, and if I see Allegra, I'm going to strangle her on the spot for spreading those lies.

"What did he want?" Mikhail asks.

I'm not sure if I should tell him. He already looks half-mad, and even though he's speaking to me, he follows Marcus with his gaze, as if he plans on going after him. The crowd around us has gone utterly quiet, and everyone is looking in our direction, whispering to each other. Dear God, could people be thinking the same things Marcus said? I place my palm on Mikhail's cheek to bring his attention to me.

"He just asked about some gossip. Forget it."

Mikhail throws a look at the people staring at us, some of them even within listening distance, who are visibly eager to overhear our conversation.

He looks down at me. "*What gossip?*" he signs.

I grin. "*You are so sexy when you sign, husband.*"

"*Don't change the subject. I know you two were engaged.*"

Oh, Nonna Giulia and her big mouth. "*We were never engaged. He wanted to marry me. I said no.*"

"*He touched you.*" Mikhail is signing so fast, I'm barely able to follow. "*If he touches you again, I'm going to end him.*"

"*He will never make that mistake again.*" I touch his chest before continuing. "*There is only one man I want to touch me. No need to be jealous.*"

I see the corner of his lips lift a little. That's good.

"Is that so?"

"*Yes.*"

We should put a stop to the idiotic rumors that Mikhail is keeping me against my will. Right away. I raise my eyebrows, grab a fistful of his shirt, rise onto my tiptoes, and lift my chin. Mikhail regards me. He's still angry. I see it in his eye, and the way he's gritting his teeth. I sigh and place my palms on either side of his face. My beautiful, dark husband. Can't he see how crazy I am for him?

"Kiss me," I utter.

His nostrils flare, and the next moment, he crashes his lips to mine. Someone gasps behind me, but I just wind my arms around Mikhail's neck and block out everything, and everyone, else. Let the fuckers watch, we'll give them better material for the rumor mill.

"Get a room, you two," Nonna Giulia says, passing us by.

I smile against Mikhail's lips.

"Good advice." He bends, scoops me into his arms, and carries me away from the crowd.

As we reach the gate, I look over his shoulder and find

most of the guests watching our retreating forms. Allegra's face is among them, horrified. I smile and wave at her.

When we get to the car, Mikhail opens the passenger door, places me on the seat, and then just stares at me. Based on his white-knuckled grip on the door, he's still furious. His arm shakes with the strength of his hold, and I can almost imagine the metal cracking under his grip.

"How many men have asked you to marry them so far?" he asks through clenched teeth.

I bite my lower lip, wondering how to reply. If I take his question literally, then none. But if he means how many men asked my father for my hand in marriage over the past two years, he won't like the answer. As a capo's daughter, I was considered quite a catch. I said no each time, of course. Half of them I haven't even met, and most of them were Father's business associates. Father wasn't pleased when I systematically rejected each of his partners, but Milene was still a minor then, so he couldn't use her as blackmail.

Slowly, I lift my right hand with three fingers up, and Mikhail's eye widens. I bite my lip harder, then add my other hand, all five fingers splayed wide.

"Eight?" he inhales and closes his eye.

I lean forward, wrap my hand around his arm and place a kiss on his tightly pressed lips. He's hot when he is mad.

"Make sure you never slip and tell me any of their names," he says against my lips, then grabs the back of my neck and devours my mouth angrily, and I feel myself getting wet again. Drenched and ready. I slide my hand down his chest until I reach his crotch and feel his hard cock under the fabric of his pants. Smiling against his lips, I stroke him lightly, enjoying the strangled sound leaving his mouth.

My fingers find the top button of his pants and, without breaking the kiss, I undo it and pull down the zipper. The parking lot is empty, everyone is still at the party. But just in case, I throw a quick look over Mikhail's shoulder before pulling out his cock. His lips go still against mine, but when I move forward on the seat and hook my legs around him, he growls.

His hands land on the inside of my thighs, then slowly move up my legs and around to grip my ass, and pull me toward him a few inches until I feel the tip of his cock at my entrance. If someone told me only a month ago I would be having sex in the middle of a parking lot, not fifty feet from two hundred people, I would have deemed them crazy. I guess I didn't quite know myself then. Taking Mikhail's lower lip between my teeth, I wrap my hands around his neck and tighten my legs around him. A moan escapes my mouth when his hard length thrusts inside me, stretching me in the best possible way. Filling me completely. I place another kiss on his mouth, grab the side of the seat, and lean back without removing my eyes from his.

What if someone comes by? Yes, it would probably create a scandal of epic proportions, but it only makes me want this more. I smile and open my legs wider. Mikhail doesn't look even marginally disturbed at the possibility of someone discovering us as he withdraws and then buries himself inside of me with such force all breath leaves my lungs. I moan and throw my head back, gripping the seat with all my might as he pounds into me again and again.

Chapter fifteen

Mikhail

I lean my shoulder on the pillar and watch Bianca and her mother as they try on shoes in a store across from me.

Bianca decided to go shopping with her and asked me if I wanted to tag along, but since I'm not a fan of her family, excluding Milene, I declined and sent Denis with her. There was a ton of work to be done anyway, so I planned on spending the morning in my office. It took barely an hour for me to lose it, grab my keys, and drive to the mall. I've been following them at a safe distance for almost three hours while they visited multiple stores and went for coffee.

I couldn't stomach the idea of Bianca being ogled at by other men at the mall, and not being there to stop them. Every fucking second I spent sitting at my desk, I kept imagining some guy approaching my wife and openly flirting with her. It wasn't the fact I thought she would welcome it. I know her well enough to be sure she wouldn't. Still, the thought of some other man talking to her drives me insane. It wasn't even a month ago when I suggested to Sergei he should visit a shrink, but now, it looks like I might be the one who needs counseling.

Bianca and her mother move to another part of the store and peruse some bags displayed on a wall, so I take a step to the side to keep them in my sight. Denis is standing by the exit, while a few paces on his left is another man in a suit, probably Chiara's security detail. The store attendant—a male employee—approaches Bianca and tries to start a conversation with her, but she only smiles and walks away. I grind my teeth and continue watching her, trying to subdue the urge to march into the store, throw her over my shoulder, and take her away.

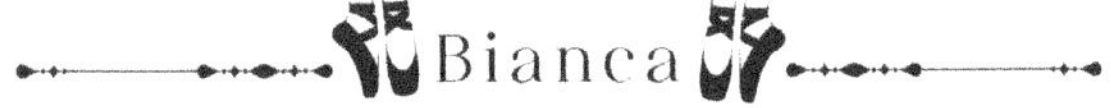

"You didn't have to make a scene, you know," my mother says as she tries one of the purses. "Everybody, and I mean everybody, talked about you two and the exit you made. It was distasteful."

I smile, take one of the larger purses, and start admiring it. If she knew what happened in the parking lot afterward, she'd have a heart attack.

"Of course, Magda had to come over right away to tell me how this kind of thing was to be expected since you're living with a Russian now, and they're not as civilized as people should be. I hate that woman." She puts the purse back on the wall rack and turns to me. "I think Bruno made a mistake by agreeing to have you marry that man. You're too sophisticated and tender for the likes of him. Do you know what people are calling you two? The beauty and the beast. It's fitting. I guess you two are having sex. I don't understand how you can let him touch you."

I gape at her for a second, then start looking through my bag for my phone. My mother's knowledge of sign language is too limited to understand what I have to tell her. As soon as my hand grips the phone, I take it out, type, and show her the screen.

We have sex every day and I can assure you it's the best fucking sex I ever had. As for touching, I enjoy touching my husband immensely and even more so when he's the one doing the touching. Especially intimately. Mikhail has very skilled fingers and an even more skilled mouth. But most of all, I love when he takes me against the wall, and I usually can't walk after that.

Her eyes widen more and more as she is reading, and then she thrusts the phone into my hand as if it burned her. "You do not speak of such things to your mother, Bianca." She squeezes her temples and shakes her head.

I start typing again, and when I'm done, I take her hand and smash the phone onto her palm, screen facing upward.

And tell Allegra if she keeps spreading lies about my husband, I will tell everyone I know she has implants in her butt and breasts. I took pictures of the doctor's report I found on her desk. Just one more word and I'm sending them to all her friends. Tell her that.

I knew those photos would come in handy one day. Allegra has been cultivating the image of a natural beauty. So, her friends finding out she came home from Brazil with much more than just a tan a few years ago would be social suicide.

"You wouldn't dare."

"*Try me,*" I sign.

My mother looks at me in surprise. "You really like him."

I sigh. There's no point in telling her I'm in love with my husband. My mother always had problems with understanding emotions, and I accepted the fact a long time ago.

We spend a few more minutes checking out the purses and then move on to the next store, where Mom picks up a couple of dresses and heads into a changing room to try them on. While I wait for her, I take out my phone, trying to ignore the guy who's been sizing me up from the other side of the store since we came in. I'm used to men looking at me. It happens all the time, but it doesn't mean I like it. Just because I'm pretty doesn't mean it's okay for a random man to ogle my ass.

I'm scrolling through my phone when I feel a hand land on my waist. I squeeze the handles of my bag and turn around, ready to smash the idiot in his head with it, but I find Mikhail standing before me.

"I guess I should announce myself next time, or risk bodily harm." His mouth curves up slightly.

I drop my phone into my bag. "*Maybe.*" I grin. "*I thought you were working.*"

"I tried." He places his hand at the back of my neck. "I kept imagining men trailing after you like they were following a beacon. I couldn't concentrate. I couldn't think about anything else. It's maddening, Bianca."

"*So, you've been stalking me around the mall?*"

"Yes."

"*How long?*"

"Three hours."

"*You have a problem, you know?*"

"Yes, I do." He bends down and whispers, "Some guys were watching you when you were trying dresses on earlier.

When you came out of the changing room, they were eating you with their eyes and I had to intervene."

My eyes widen. "*Are they alive?*"

"I threw them out when you weren't looking. I won't be so gentle next time." He places his hand on my chin and tilts my head up. "No one is allowed to look at my wife the way they were doing."

I close my eyes for a moment to compose myself because this is seriously turning me on. Should I be worried about the fact I find his possessiveness hot? I am all for feminism and emancipation, and I feel rather guilty because just the thought of Mikhail scaring men away for looking at me starts a tingling sensation between my legs.

"*And what would you do if one of them tried to touch me?*" I sign. "*Or kiss me?*"

Mikhail's lips tighten, his eye staring at me, as he bends until his mouth comes next to my ear. "If anyone dared to touch you, I would chop off their hand. Like I should have done with that idiot at your Nonna's birthday party," he whispers. "And if someone was insane enough to try putting his mouth near my wife, I would behead him."

I suck in my breath as I feel myself getting wet.

"Bianca, do you think this color works with my hair?" My mom exits the changing room, and surprise spreads on her face at seeing Mikhail there. "Mr. Orlov. Did something happen?"

"*Yes,*" I sign quickly before he can reply. "*We have to go. I'll call you tomorrow.*"

Grabbing Mikhail's hand, I drag him out of the store and toward the narrow hallway on the right, where I saw the restrooms.

"Care to share what just happened to make us run from the boutique?" he asks once we're far enough away not to be overheard.

I turn around to make sure no one is around, pull my skirt up, and tug his hand so it presses against my wet panties. Mikhail inhales sharply as he massages me with his palm, making me whimper. Without removing his hand, he takes a step forward and then another, guiding me backward until my back hits the wall.

"It looks like you missed me." He moves my panties to the side and places his finger at my entrance. "Did you, little lamb?"

I nod, put my hands on his chest, and slide them down until they reach his crotch.

"Good," he whispers, then crashes his mouth to mine at the same time he thrusts his finger deep inside me. "Here? Or home?"

Based on the sound of his voice and how hard his cock is under my palm, he doesn't like the home option any more than I do.

"Here," I whisper, not quite believing what I'm saying.

Mikhail grabs me by my thighs and lifts me. I wrap my legs around his waist, put my arms around his neck, and trail kisses down his neck as he walks to the ladies' restroom on the left. After a quick check of the stalls, he locks the door and carries me toward the wide marble counter with sinks.

I squirm as the bare skin of my backside connects with the cold stone, but the unpleasant sensation is quickly forgotten because I am too focused on removing my panties.

"You've fucked with my head so completely, Bianca." He

grabs my hips and buries himself inside me in one swift motion. "I can't think straight anymore."

This. The feeling of him filling me so completely makes me want to scream in delight. There is nothing better. Mikhail's cock is huge, just like the rest of him, and I enjoy the sensation of my walls stretching to accommodate his size. Placing his hand at the back of my neck, he slides out slowly, then slams back into me. I gasp. Then smile.

"Harder," I urge.

The hand at the back of my neck moves upward, grabbing a handful of hair.

"Like this?" he asks, and slams into me again.

"Yes." I grip the side of the marble counter with all my strength, wrap my legs around his hips and lean back as Mikhail destroys me, piece by little piece. And the destruction has never felt better.

Chapter sixteen

Bianca

When Mikhail told me we were having dinner with the pakhan's wife, I expected a detached, perfectly dressed Russian woman who, most likely, would ignore me the entire evening. Nina Petrova is the complete opposite of what I anticipated, in her torn jeans, flowing blouse, and a small silver nose ring.

"Don't you dare, Roman. I mean it!" Nina pokes her husband's chest, staring daggers at him, then turns to me. "He's been following me around the house for two months like I'm going to trip over my feet and fall down the stairs as if I'm some baby deer."

She takes my hand and leads me across the large foyer toward the hallway on the right side of the house.

"We'll be in the kitchen. Mikhail said Bianca has a mean recipe for pasta, so maybe she'll share it with Igor," Nina calls over her shoulder. "If I see you anywhere near the east wing, I'm going to end you, Roman."

It's rather funny, seeing this petite woman threatening

her hulk of a husband. Petrov doesn't say a thing as he stands there, leaning on his cane, and watches us leave.

"Since I told him I'm pregnant, Roman has become unbearable with his mother hen behavior," she says while we walk down the hallway. "So, you and Mikhail . . . how's it going with you two?"

I just smile a little and nod. Usually, people who meet me for the first time tend to keep quiet as if there's no point in starting a conversation. Nina isn't like that at all. It's . . . strangely refreshing.

"Okay, now, please try to keep an open mind. It's not as bad as it looks," she says and opens the double doors in front of us.

The first thing I hear is a deep voice yelling in Russian, then two more female voices joining the yelling match, followed by a sound of clanking silverware. I enter the kitchen after Nina and stop in my tracks, staring.

A huge man in his sixties, wearing a white apron and standing in front of the stove, is motioning to the black smoke billowing out of the oven and shouting at the girl on the other side of the kitchen island. Behind him, another girl is hitting his back with a rag. And in the corner, an older woman with short gray hair is yelling at the cook while threatening him with a spoon dripping with sauce.

"We have a guest!" Nina shouts, and everyone turns toward us." This is Bianca, Mikhail's wife. Be nice."

They look at me, nod, and return to their yelling.

"Well, it was worth a try. Sorry." Nina shrugs.

I take the phone from my purse, type in the message window, and show the screen to Nina.

"Oh, we're not intruding. This is just an ordinary day in

the kitchen. Don't worry. Let's go to Varya, so you can write the pasta recipe for her, and she'll check if we have the ingredients. Since Valentina burned the meat again, we'll need a backup dish. You can instruct Igor on how to make it, if that's okay?"

I look at her, confused. How does she mean for me to instruct the cook? I doubt he's familiar with sign language. I guess Nina notices the confused look on my face because she waves with her hand dismissively.

"Don't worry. Igor only speaks Russian, anyway. Just point with your finger. It works for me—most of the time, at least."

"Did you talk with Dushku?" I ask Roman and take a sip of whiskey.

"Yes. He says he had nothing to do with the shooting, or with the guys who followed you."

"And you believe him?"

"I'm not sure." Roman leans back in his chair and grinds his teeth. "Everything about this is fucked. All of the guys were Albanians, but none of them were working for Dushku. They were just some random gang members. What I am sure about is that the same person hired all of them."

"Maybe it's a setup to make us attack the Albanians. We have the product, Albanians buy it. If we start a war with them and cut the supply, the Albanians will have to search elsewhere."

"Irish?" He raises his eyebrows.

"Nope. Italians."

"It doesn't make sense. Why did the don agree to the cease-fire, and the marriage to unite La Cosa Nostra and the Bratva if they were planning to make a deal with the Albanians anyway?"

"To buy some time." I take out my phone and start browsing the photos. "I found it strange Bianca's brother wasn't at the wedding. They're close. It didn't make any sense. When I asked her where he was, she said Bruno sent him to arrange some business and he still isn't back. Take a guess where he is."

"Oh, I have a feeling I won't like the answer."

I open the photo our contact in Mexico sent me this morning and pass the phone to Roman.

"Son of a bitch," he says, staring at the screen.

"Yep. Bruno's son and Mendoza, our main supplier."

"Looks like the Italians framed the Albanians, or tried to at least, so we'd turn on each other. Most likely, they're hoping to swoop in and offer to supply the drugs to the Albanians the moment our business dealings ended."

"Yes. But I think this is all Bruno's doing. He enjoys licking the don's ass. I believe he planned to inform him only after he'd set the events in motion."

"Well, we're not going to war with the Albanians, so Bruno will end up with a lot of product and no buyer."

"I'm sure Don Agostini won't be happy with Bruno going behind his back," I say. "Especially since the don himself agreed to the treaty between us."

"You know, I always wondered why Bruno offered his daughter for the marriage."

"He wanted exclusive inside info on the Bratva. Bianca told me so herself."

"Oh? Did she now?"

"Yes. She said no. I have a silent alarm set on the door to my home office. Bianca's never tried to get inside, Roman."

"Are you sure?" He looks at me sideways. "Absolutely sure?"

"I am. Why, do you doubt my judgment?"

"Of course, I do. You're desperately in love with her, anyone can see that."

I look at the glass in my hand. The light is reflecting in the dark brown liquid much the same as it does in Bianca's eyes.

"I am," I say and down the drink.

Roman smiles and shakes his head. "Well, I'll be damned! If someone told me a woman would have you, of all people, wrapped around her finger in less than a month, I would've considered them mad."

"You're one to talk. Remind me how much time it took Nina to have you eating out of her hand?"

"Way more than a month."

"You were a goner after a week, Roman."

"Okay, two weeks." He shrugs. "And what about Bianca?"

"What about her?"

"Does she feel the same?"

"I don't know. Bianca is hard to read."

"Women are hard to read in general, Mikhail. Sometimes, I feel they came from another fucking planet."

"I think she likes spending time with me." I shrug. "We went to the mall last week."

"I knew it." Roman hits the chair with his palm. "She dragged you to watch some teen movie. Admit it!"

"Not exactly. We had sex in the restroom."

"Mikhail Orlov. Had sex in the restroom." He raises his eyebrows. "In a *mall*!"

"Yes," I say, and he bursts out laughing.

I ignore him and continue, "She also said she wanted me to take her dancing."

"You? Dancing? What's next, pigs flying?" Roman sighs. "Did you tell your wife what you do for the Bratva?"

"She knows I'm in charge of distribution."

"So, you haven't told her."

I look down at my glass. "Nope."

"She'll find out, sooner or later, you know this."

"She won't. I'll make sure she never finds out."

"Mikhail . . ."

"She doesn't care about my eye. Or the scars. I don't know why, but she doesn't. She's never asked what happened, even though I know she must wonder. But I can't tell her what I do for the Bratva . . . I don't think she'd be able to get past that."

"Well, shit." He squeezes his temples. "Okay, I'll talk with Maxim, maybe he can take over . . ."

"No. Information extraction is my job. And anyway, who could be a better interrogator than someone who's experienced most of the torture techniques himself?"

"Oh my God, this is amazing." Nina moans and reaches with her fork toward the pot again.

The big cook, who is standing on the other side of the

table, grabs the pot by the handle and slides it toward himself, speaking something in Russian and pointing behind his back.

"Baby wants it." Nina grabs the other handle of the pot and starts pulling it back to her.

The cook lets go of the pot, throws his hands in the air, and walks away.

"Baby card works every time. Igor doesn't understand much, but he knows that word." Nina grins, takes another forkful of the pasta, and stuffs it in her mouth.

I can't help but laugh, grab another fork and join her.

A throat clears behind me, and I turn to find Mikhail pulling up a chair and sitting next to me.

"Is this our dinner?" He quirks a brow. "The one the four of us should be eating together? In the dining room?"

I put down the fork. *"Nina started it. I had to join. It would be rude to let the pakhan's wife eat alone."*

"I see . . ." He cocks his head a little and leans toward me. "Can I have a taste?"

I smile, take a little bit of the pasta on the fork, and lift it to his mouth. Nina's watching the whole exchange from the other side of the table with wide eyes, her mouth gaping open.

"Holy shit," she mumbles, but Mikhail ignores her comment.

"You made it? I thought they invited you to dinner, not to make one."

"Well, technically, Igor made it," Nina throws in. "Bianca instructed him, and I helped with the translation."

"I wonder how that worked out."

"I pointed. And Nina poked Igor in the ribs when he didn't follow."

Mikhail raises his hand to brush his finger down my cheek and his lips widen a little in a smile. It's small and gone after a second, but my heart still skips a beat. He has a beautiful smile.

The kitchen door on the other side of the room opens and the pakhan comes in, his face somber. He says something in Russian and Mikhail curses.

"There was a fire in one of the warehouses. I have to go." He kisses the top of my head and stands up. "I'll call Denis to pick you up and take you home."

"Message me so I know you're okay. Please."

"I will." The look he gives me is part surprise and part satisfaction, and then he's gone.

It's close to three in the morning when Mikhail comes back. I jump up from the couch the moment I hear the door open and, clutching the blanket around me, rush to him. He's covered in soot, black splotches all over his hands and face, but he looks unharmed.

"Why aren't you sleeping?"

"I was worried."

"Lena?"

"Asleep. We had pancakes for dinner again." I sign and start unbuttoning his shirt. The sleeve is torn in one place, but when I inspect his upper arm, I don't find any injuries.

"The pants. Then the shower."

He doesn't complain about me ordering him around, just kisses me lightly on the lips and, leaving the ruined suit on the floor, heads toward the bathroom. I take his shirt and pants to the trash can, then go after him.

In the bathroom, I remove my clothes and get into the shower where Mikhail is already washing his hair. I take the soap from the shelf, lather my hands, and lift them to his face. He looks down at me for a second, then bends his head. There's a big black stain on his right cheek, so I start there. It comes off rather easily, and I move on to his forehead and then his neck. There's no soot on his chest, but I move my hands there anyway, stroking his skin in a circular motion.

Mikhail takes a step forward and places his hands on the tiles on either side of my head, caging me between his body and the shower wall. I slide my hand lower and grip his hard cock, enjoying the way his breathing quickens.

"Not yet," he says in my ear and, taking me by my hips, turns me around so I'm facing the wall.

His hands move slowly down my stomach until they stop between my legs, and I feel his finger teasing at my entrance.

"You are the most beautiful thing I've ever set eyes on," he whispers and thrusts one finger inside me, then adds another, and I gasp silently. "And you, my little sunray, are as beautiful on the inside, as you are on the outside."

When he curls his fingers inside of me, pressing the sensitive spot near my clit, a shudder rocks my whole body so hard I have to press my forehead and palms against the wall to keep myself standing.

"Mine," he says against my neck, winds his free arm

around my midsection, and lifts me without removing his fingers from inside my pussy.

I'm panting, not able to inhale enough air, as Mikhail carries me into his bedroom with my back pressed to his chest and my head thrown back onto his shoulder. It amazes me how he easily manages to carry my whole weight with only one arm, while his other hand is still buried inside of me, teasing me.

The moment he sets me down and removes his fingers, I turn and push him down onto the bed, then crawl over his huge body and sit down on his cock. It feels like home, and I come the second he fills me up, wishing so much I could scream his name at that moment.

I keep riding him, marveling at the feel of his hands on my waist and his cock straining against my still-tingling walls. Mikhail groans and starts pounding into me from below, while I clutch at his shoulders so hard he'll probably end up with nail marks. When I feel myself coming again, I arch my back and let out a barely audible scream. The next moment, Mikhail explodes inside me.

He's still panting when I lean forward. I gently touch my nose to his and bury my hands in his hair, looking into his mismatched eyes. In my chest, my heart leaps with joy every time he's near, making me feel complete instead of the flawed, lost person I've always believed myself to be. I remember Marcus calling me an ice princess once because I didn't want to cuddle or hold hands in public. He made it sound like a joke, but I know he meant it.

It's different with Mikhail. There's an inexplicable urge to touch him that consumes me whenever he's around, as if my body is somehow drawn to him like a magnet. It scares me a little. Dancing was the only thing that kept me sane, so when the injury ended my career, I thought my life was over. I wanted it back, so much, and I never thought I'd want anything more. Until now.

Mikhail pulls himself up on his elbows and tilts his head to the side, watching me. "What is it, dusha moya?"

I bend to place my lips on his forehead, then his left eye, but when I move to his right one, he turns his head to the side, avoiding my lips.

He's really sensitive about his eye, but no, I won't let him do that.

"Mikhail . . ." I rasp, but he just shakes his head.

"Please, don't."

"Why?"

"Because my eye is hideous. I don't want your lips anywhere near it."

I grind my teeth and take his face in my hands. "It's not," I whisper.

Mikhail just looks at me and smiles a little. It hits me right in the chest—his impossibly sad smile.

"Okay," he says and places a finger over my lips. "Please, stop hurting yourself because of me. You promised you wouldn't do that anymore." Another sad smile. "Come here, it's late. Let's sleep."

He's in love with me. I know it without him telling me so. It's visible in his every single act. Why won't he let me love him back, then? My dark, dangerous husband—so strong, so unbreakable, and so heartbreakingly alone, even with me next to him. I don't know why he won't let me in or why he is still hiding from me. Even after I've seen him naked numerous times, he still wears long-sleeved shirts when I'm around during the day. Doesn't he understand no one will ever compare to him in my eyes? How can I make him get that through his thick head?

He embraces me, reaches out toward the bedside lamp, and turns it off. It's not a particularly meaningful thing, and I don't know why, but him turning off the lamp is the last straw for me. I decide I've had enough. Enough of everyone being shocked by the fact I like him, enough of people telling me there's something wrong with me, but most of all I'm done with him thinking he's not good enough and denying my touch. I sit up, grab the lamp, turn the damn thing back on, and spin around to face Mikhail.

"This stops now. I will touch you wherever and whenever I want. If I want to kiss you, you don't have the right to turn your head."

Mikhail pulls himself onto his elbows and regards me with his mouth pressed into a thin line. "Baby . . ."

"No. Do not 'baby' me now. Sweet talk won't get you anywhere this time."

"Sweet talk?" he raises an eyebrow.

"No more pulling away. No more hot and cold. No more long sleeves." I point my finger at him. *"If I see you in another long-sleeved shirt around the house, I'm going to tear it off you."*

Mikhail is very good at keeping emotions from showing on his face, but I catch the surprise flashing in his eye as he tilts his head and watches me.

I don't care if I first met him only a month ago. I don't care our marriage was arranged as a business deal without my say in the matter. I. Don't. Care. He's mine, and I'll fight anything and anyone who tries to keep him from me, even if it's Mikhail himself.

"And I get to kiss you everywhere. You got that? I will draw it for you, if needed. Everywhere. Yes, your eye is fucked. I want to kiss it anyway." I grind my teeth and stare him down. *"And you are going to let me."* I poke him with my finger in the center of his chest, then continue, *"Because I am in love with you. Every part of you. Your grumpy personality included. Fucking deal with it."*

I take a deep breath, cross my arms, and watch him as he stares at me without blinking. He's so still that, for a moment, I wonder if he stopped breathing, then he suddenly lunges at me, and I find myself on my back with Mikhail's body sprawled over mine. He still doesn't say anything, just presses his palms on either side of my face and bends his head until our noses touch. His right thumb traces the contour of my cheek and chin, and then comes to rest on my lips.

"Tell me again," he whispers, regarding me carefully, like a hawk, as if he's searching for some deception. I look at him right in the eyes and hold his gaze, willing him to see what I'm saying is true.

"I am . . . so in love . . . with you," I say, and the next second, Mikhail's mouth crashes down on mine.

His arms come around my back as he rolls, taking me with him until I'm laying atop him, never breaking the kiss. He's squeezing me into him so tightly it's hard to breathe.

"Ya lyublyu tebya vsey dushoy, solnyshko," he says into my ear. *"Ya ne pozvolyu nikomu zabrat' tebya."*

I smile and lean in to kiss his left eyebrow. Then I move to the right side of his face and trace my finger down the line of the thickest scar, from the top of his forehead, all the way to his chin.

"You are . . . so badass . . . husband." I kiss his right eyebrow, then the corner of his right eye. He doesn't move away. I kiss it again.

"And you are so crazy, dusha moya." He sighs.

"Only . . . for you . . . Mikhail."

He places his finger on my lips. "Enough. Stop hurting yourself."

I smile and slide my hand down his chest. "Make . . . me."

Chapter seventeen

Mikhail

I READ THE MESSAGE FROM OUR CONTACT IN MEXICO and call Roman right away.

"Angelo Scardoni is moving the product," I say the moment he answers the call. "What do you want me to do?"

"Do you have an ETA on when they'll cross the border?"

"Sometime Thursday night."

"Find a good spot to intercept them after they cross. Blow them up."

"Are you sure?"

"Bruno torched down my warehouse. Anton is still in the hospital with third-degree burns. I want the product gone."

"All right."

"And make sure they know it was us," Roman says and ends the call.

I put my phone back into my pocket, take a chair and place it in front of a man sitting with his hands and legs tied in the middle of the room. His palms are turned up, showing his red, blistered skin.

I sit down, lean back, and regard the Italian asshole in front of me. Early twenties, a bit overweight, and is wearing jeans and a designer T-shirt. He doesn't look like a foot soldier. Probably someone's nephew—a few steps removed and looking for a way to rise in rank by taking on the job of burning down the Bratva's warehouse. Idiot. And based on the way his eyes are staring at me—huge and unblinking—is scared shitless.

"So, you like burning things, Enzo?" I nod toward his burned hands. "You need more practice."

He's mumbling something I can't understand through the gag in his mouth. Doesn't matter, he's not ready to give me the information I need. Not yet. I'm giving him fifteen minutes tops.

"Burned skin hurts like a bitch. Just the lightest touch and the pain pierces you all the way to the spine. Let me show you." I lean in to press my thumb lightly in the middle of Enzo's palm.

He jumps in the chair so hard he almost topples to the side, and there's a wheezing sound coming through the rag in his mouth, like an animal caught in a snare.

"You know, I really hate torturing people," I say. "It's time-consuming and messy and, in the end, everyone talks. It would be nice if we could skip the messy part because blood is a bitch to wash away. Do you know how many of my suits have ended up in the trash this month? Four." I lean my elbows on my knees and regard him. "I like this suit, Enzo. I'd appreciate it if you would just tell me what I need to know, and I'll let you go. Simple as that."

I take one of the smaller knives lined up on the metal table next to me and pointedly examine the blade. When I turn toward Enzo and put the tip of the knife above his palm, he starts fighting the restraints like a madman. He's shaking his head, trying to say something, but I ignore his thrashing and slash his burned skin in a long diagonal line across his palm. He manages to scream even with the gag pressed into his mouth. I lean back in my chair again, take a sip from the water bottle I keep on the table, and wait for him to calm down.

Enzo stops thrashing after a minute or so and sags in his chair, breathing heavily through his nose. I wait for a few more minutes, then reach for a box of matches on the other side of the table.

"So, we've tested touch and the knife so far." I take one match out, light it up and hold it in front of Enzo's face. "You think that was painful?"

He nods his head and starts to cry.

"It's nothing compared to having an open flame touching skin that's already burned."

A wet stain appears on Enzo's jeans while he watches the burning match, his eyes bloodshot. I let go of the match, and it falls in the puddle of piss on the floor between Enzo's feet, missing his hand by just a few inches.

"Well, looks like my sight is not what it once was." I sigh. "Good thing we have a whole box."

I reach for the box of matches again, take out another one, then look up at Enzo.

"Or, maybe, we could talk now? Tell me, Enzo, how much time do you think's passed since I came in? An hour? More maybe?" I light the match and raise my hand. "It's been eight minutes. Time passes slowly when you're in pain. So, here's what we'll do. I'll remove the gag. You'll talk. If I think you are lying or leaving anything out, I put the gag back and it will stay on for two more hours. You don't want to be in the same room with me for two hours, Enzo."

I lean forward until my face is right in front of his.

"You see, I haven't even started with you yet. This was just the two of us getting to know each other, and me gauging your pain threshold. It's really low, Enzo. This means I'd probably start with your nails, then move on to your fingers and teeth. I assume it would take the two hours I mentioned, and I'm sure you'll sing like a bird when I take the gag off after that. But you won't have any fingers or teeth left then. I think you should take the deal I'm offering."

He sniffs and nods.

"Good choice." I blow out the match and stand up to remove Enzo's gag.

He starts talking the moment his mouth is free.

Ten minutes later, I leave the room, and while walking across the empty warehouse, I take out my phone to call Roman.

"The arsonist talked. It was Bruno. He orchestrated everything," I say, "And they took the drugs from Diego Rivera, not Mendoza."

"That son of a bitch. When I asked Diego to double the quantities for us, he said he's already stretched too thin."

"From what Enzo said, it looks like police killed Manny Sandoval, and Diego Rivera took over his business. That's how he got more product."

"Fuck!" he curses. "There's always some shit going on down there."

"Yeah. And we have another problem." I squeeze the

bridge of my nose and sigh. "We can't blow the transport, Roman."

"Why the hell not?"

"Bruno decided to deliver a gift to Dushku along with the product. There's a girl on the truck."

"Are you shitting me? That's not Dushku's style."

"It was meant to be a surprise."

"Your father-in-law is one sick son of a bitch."

"Yeah. Now what?"

"Put someone on their tail. When they stop for the night, get the girl out and then blow the thing up."

"Okay."

I put the phone back in my pocket, get into the car, and start the engine.

Bianca

"I don't like clubs, Bianca."

"Please? I promised Milene." I make a sad expression. *"And you said you would take me dancing, remember?"*

Milene's friend, Caterina, wanted to go somewhere for her birthday. My sister proposed Ural, one of the Bratva's clubs. I told her it's not wise, even with the truce between the two sides. But she insisted, saying if Mikhail and I come along, nothing would happen. If Father finds out, she's screwed.

"I said, we'll see," he says and passes his hand through my hair. "When?"

"Tonight." I smile. *"I've already arranged with Sisi to look after Lena. She'll be here any moment."*

"So, you were sure I would say yes." He bends until our heads are at the same level. "Roman was right. You have wrapped me around your little finger."

"*Is that bad?*" I ask and watch as he takes my hand in his and places the tip of my pinkie to his lips.

"Nope." He kisses my finger. "Who else is coming?"

"*Milene and Caterina. And Andrea, the don's granddaughter. Maybe her sister, Isabella, as well.*"

"Rossi's new wife?" He lifts his eyebrow. "I'll call Pavel to let him know. We'll need more security."

Too loud music, too many people, too much alcohol. I never liked clubs when I was younger, and now I just loath them. Everybody knows that, and once Pavel spreads the news of me coming to Ural with Bianca, I'll never hear the end of it.

I lead the girls to the table in the corner and turn around, making sure all four security guards arranged by Pavel are in their places. Combined with Andrea's and Isabella's bodyguards, it makes seven men watching over four girls. Deeming it more than enough, I take Bianca's hand and pull her to the side near the end of the bar where there's more light.

"So, what do you think?"

"*I love it.*" She beams at me. "*Very chic.*"

"Pavel likes to overdo things." I place my hand at the back of her neck and tilt her head up. "The only reason I've come to this club is because you asked me to. I hate them. And that loathing is becoming exponentially stronger with every second."

Bianca narrows her eyes at me as her hand lifts to trace the shape of a question mark on my chest. I love when she does that.

"Because I notice every man who looks at you, and there are at least fifty of them here," I say, then bend my head to whisper in her ear. "I'm afraid someone may try to take you from me, and I have this compulsion to kill them all before they have a chance to give it a try."

Sighing, Bianca climbs onto the barstool behind her, takes my face between her palms, and pulls me toward her until I'm standing between her legs. She touches her nose to mine and starts caressing my face with her hands while holding my gaze, unblinking. She starts with my chin, tenderly moves over my cheeks, then buries her fingers into my hair. I close my eyes and let myself drown in the warmth of her touch, forgetting about the people around us. A kiss lands at the right side of my chin, just over the thickest scar. I still find it unexpected, the way she touches my ruined face, with so much affection. Another kiss, at the tip of my nose this time, and I feel my lips curve into a smile. The next kiss lands at the corner of my mouth, then on my left cheek. I keep my eyes closed, waiting for what will be next. The left eyebrow. Then my right cheek. Tip of my nose again. My mouth widens even more.

"You are . . ." a soft whisper right next to my ear, "so beautiful . . . when you smile."

I squeeze my arms tighter around her and brush my cheek against hers. My silly little sunray.

"No one . . ." another whisper, "compares to . . .you."

Her hands wrap around my neck, and I feel her breath near my ear as she moves her mouth even closer. "I love you . . . Mikhail."

I press my face into Bianca's neck and take a deep breath, inhaling her scent. She has no idea what hearing her say my name does to me. It breaks me and puts me back together every single time. Each touch from her melts my insides.

"If you knew how crazy in love with you I am," I say into her neck, "you'd be scared shitless, Bianca."

She pulls away a little, so she can look me in the eyes, smiles, and nudges my nose with hers. "Never," she mouths then crashes her lips to mine.

Chapter eighteen

Bianca

THE PHONE HAS BEEN ON THE COUNTER IN FRONT of me, with a message window open, for five minutes. I exchanged numbers with Nina when we went to the pakhan's place the other night, and I've been planning on messaging her for several days now, but I'm not sure if she'll want to answer my questions. We're not exactly friends, but I have no one else to ask, other than Mikhail. I'm pretty sure he'd tell me if I asked him directly, but if my suspicions are correct, I don't want to make him talk about it. I take the phone and start typing.

19:09 Bianca: Hey. It's Bianca. Are you busy?

19:11 Nina: Well, I don't think keeping my head above the toilet since six a.m., constitutes as being busy. Lol. It's no fun, that's for sure. You know how they say the morning sickness lasts only for two months? THEY LIED! I've been puking since the 3rd week, and the "morning" part is not true either.

You two want to come over for a coffee or something? How's Grumpy doing?

I look at the last line and snort.

19:14 Bianca: Mikhail's still at work. Does he know you call him Grumpy?

19:14 Nina: Of course, he does. He doesn't come here often but when he does, he usually sits in the corner and broods.

19:15 Bianca: Yeah, he does that a lot. I wanted to ask you something. It's about Mikhail. But if you are not comfortable answering just tell me, it's okay.

19:16 Nina: Sure. Shoot.

19:16 Bianca: Do you know what happened to him?

A couple of minutes go by until Nina responds

19:18 Nina: Yes. Roman told me.

19:18 Bianca: He was tortured, wasn't he? I saw the scars, and those are not the result of an accident or something; they're too precise, almost clinical. His back is covered with whip marks. Can you please tell me who tortured my husband? And why?

19:20 Nina: It was the old pakhan. Roman's father.

I stare at her answer, shocked. Roman's father did that? The phone in my hand starts ringing. It's Nina. I take the call.

"I know you can't reply, but I think it's better if I tell you than type. It's . . . it's a really bad story, Bianca."

Nina's voice is low and strangled, so different from her usual cheerful tone, which tells me whatever she's going to say will probably be worse than I could have imagined.

"I only know what Roman told me, and he didn't go into details. I'll tell you what I know. You can tap the phone for 'yes,' okay?"

I tap the microphone with my nail.

"Promise me you won't ask Mikhail to talk about it. Ever. Please."

Yes, it's definitely worse than I thought. I tap the phone again.

"Mikhail's father handled the finances for the old pakhan. One day a lot of money went missing, just vanished from the pakhan's account. A couple of million. He concluded Mikhail's father had something to do with it, so he took his whole family into one of the old warehouses. He killed Mikhail's mother. Then he ordered his man to . . . to rape his sister. Mikhail and his father watched."

Oh, my God. My legs are shaking, and I feel as if I'm going to be sick, so I sit down on the kitchen floor and put my forehead on my knees.

"So, when Mikhail's father still couldn't say where the money was, the pakhan decided he needed a better incentive," Nina says, and from the sound of her voice, I know she's crying. "I don't know what he did to Mikhail to make his father talk, but based on what you told me, I can assume. Roman said he and Maxim found Mikhail and his family the next day. Everybody except Mikhail was dead. He was only nineteen, Bianca."

There's a buzzing sound in my ears, like a TV without a signal, canceling all other sounds around me. My vision blurs with tears, so when I stand up, I hit my hip on the counter, but I ignore the pain and rush to the guest room. I'm feeling impossibly cold, so I get in the bed under the thick blanket, still clutching the phone to my ear.

"Roman killed his father earlier that day, when he found him trying to choke Varya," she continues. "He got the details from the two men who were at the warehouse with the old pakhan. He killed them both, too. Even after all those years, he can't forgive himself for killing them and robbing Mikhail of the opportunity to do it himself."

There's a sniffing sound on the other side, then something clanging followed by a whispered curse.

"I'm feeling sick again, I'm not sure if it's from telling you this or the pregnancy. Probably both. I have to get back to my puking. If you need to know anything else, message me and I'll ask Roman. Just . . . don't ask Mikhail."

I tap at the phone and let it fall on the blanket, then bury my face into the pillow. And cry.

The door to the bedroom opens a couple hours later, but I keep my head under the blanket and pretend I'm sleeping. No way can I let Mikhail see me in this state, he'll know something happened right away. I hear his steps approach the bed, and a moment later, I feel a light kiss on the top of my head. He whispers a few words in Russian and then he's gone. I cry for another hour after he leaves, wondering how a person who went through something like Mikhail did, can be so tender and loving.

When I go into the bathroom to take a shower my face

is still red and my eyes puffy. At least it's dark now, and the swelling should be gone by morning.

The light is off when I enter our bedroom. Mikhail is lying on his side asleep, back turned toward the door. I tiptoe to the bed, get under the blanket, and place my head on the pillow, burying my face into Mikhail's neck.

"I thought you were sleeping," he says.

I reach out with my hand and stroke the length of his back, feeling the ridges along the way, then move to his stomach and the wide patch of molted skin where he was burned, and, finally, up to the long thin scar on his chest.

"I love you." My voice is so very faint, but I know he hears me, because he embraces me around my waist and crushes me against his chest.

"I'll be there in an hour," I tell Maxim and end the call.

When I exit the gym, Bianca lifts her head from her coffee and follows me with her gaze as I walk to the kitchen. I left my T-shirt in the gym, and it feels strange being in front of someone with my chest and back so casually on display. I don't think anyone's seen me shirtless for more than a decade. She watches me over the rim of her cup, her gaze traveling from my stomach and across my chest, but there's no reluctance in her eyes. Her gaze is roaming my body and based on the way the corner of her lip curls up, she likes what she sees.

I open the fridge to take out a bottle of water when there's a sudden touch at the small of my back, a finger trailing circular pattern upward across my skin, then back down along my spine. Another finger on my right bicep, traveling to my front then going down my chest. When she reaches the waistband of my sweats, she slides her hand inside to grip my cock, and leans onto my back.

"Damn, baby . . . I need to be at the pakhan's in an hour."

Bianca's hand slips into my boxer briefs and wraps around my already hard length, and at the same time, I feel her tongue on my back, licking along my spine. I snap. A growl escapes from my chest as I turn, and grabbing her around the waist, I throw her over my shoulder in a fireman's hold and run toward the bedroom.

The moment I put her down, Bianca takes the waistband of my sweats and pushes them down along with my boxer briefs. A mischievous grin spreads over her face as she pushes me onto the bed then crawls over my body to press her mouth to mine. She bites my lip, then moves lower, trailing kisses down my neck and chest, and stops when she reaches my stomach.

"Looks like our roles have been reversed this time," she signs, smirking.

"Oh? How so?"

"I still have my clothes on. And you are the one fully naked." She signs, traces the tip of her finger down my stomach and brushes my fully erect cock. *"At my mercy."*

I wonder if she realizes how true her declaration is. She could press a gun to my temple and pull the trigger, and I wouldn't move a finger to stop her. As I watch, she bends and licks the tip of my cock, and it takes a tremendous amount of control not to let myself come immediately. Another lick, circling the head of my cock, then she slowly takes it into her mouth. I suck in a breath and grab her braid which has fallen over her shoulder.

Keeping the end of the braid between my fingers, I wrap the length of it around my hand, once, twice, and then a third time until I reach the nape of her neck. Then I pull on it, until Bianca lets my cock slide from her mouth with a pop and looks up at me. I tighten my hold on her hair and watch as she arches her delicate neck. She seems so breakable, but it doesn't matter. No one will dare put a finger on her ever again, because now she has her own monster to watch over her. Placing my free hand on the side of that fragile neck, I brush the line of her chin with my thumb.

"I need my cock inside of you, baby," I say and squeeze her hair lightly, "right now."

Bianca smiles, reaches under her skirt, and in the next moment, there's the sound of material tearing. Her hand comes away, holding ruined lacy panties which she throws to the side. I keep my hand in her hair as she lowers herself onto my cock and starts riding me, still wearing her silky blouse and fancy skirt. A small sound resembling a scream leaves her lips as her walls begin spasming around my length, and my control snaps. I let go of her hair to grab her around her waist and slam her down on my cock. Bianca gasps, her hands squeezing my forearms, then she pants as I pound into her from below. Her eyes never release my gaze as her body trembles with her second, even more intense orgasm, and my seed starts filling her up. It's the most beautiful sight I've ever seen.

"This will be the first time in my life I've been late for a meeting with Roman." I look down at Bianca who's buttoning my shirt. "You're corrupting me."

She just shrugs and finishes with the last button.

"You came into the kitchen shirtless. What did you expect?"

Definitely not her jumping on me this way.

"I may stop wearing shirts around the house altogether if I can expect the same result."

"You do that. And we'll see."

"Done." I lean in and kiss her. "I have to go. I won't be back before morning."

I turn to leave but stop at hearing her say my name. It hits me in the chest whenever she does that because I know it hurts her, but she keeps on, no matter what I say.

"Be careful."

"I will." I kiss her forehead. "Message me when Lena comes back from day care."

She nods, places her hand on my chest, and traces a shape of a heart with the tip of her finger.

"I love you, too, baby." I take her face in my palms and touch my nose to hers. "You can't imagine how much."

It takes us six hours to organize everything and put all the men in place. Dimitri, Yuri, and three of the soldiers are waiting at one rest stop, while Denis, Ivan, and Kostya with two more soldiers are waiting at the second stop. We're not sure at which of those two stops Bruno's driver will choose to stay the night, so we've had to split our forces, leaving us shorthanded. Pavel had to stay behind to keep his eye on the clubs, and with Anton still at the hospital, I had to bring Sergei with me as a backup to trail the transport truck.

Having Sergei on a field mission is always a disaster just waiting to happen. He was banned from field duty last year after he blew up the whole Irish warehouse, leaving only ashes behind. I have no idea what Roman was thinking when he sent him into the field a few months back while we were fighting the Italians. The man is a fucking ticking bomb. If I didn't know already, I never would have guessed the two of them are half brothers.

No one except for Roman and Maxim knows what Sergei did before he came to the Bratva, but I have my suspicions. Everyone in our circle has to be proficient with a gun and a rifle. Sergei is proficient with every single weapon he's ever come in contact with—a sniper rifle, heavy assault rifles, even grenade launchers. He's also a specialist in all kinds of explosives—homemade and professionally made. A military-trained killing machine, probably black ops.

"Remember what we agreed on," I say. "The guys will handle the driver. You rig the truck and wait until I get the girl out. Do not deviate from the plan. And don't blow the fucking truck up while I'm still inside, Sergei."

"You're edgy tonight."

"I want to get this over with as quickly as possible. My wife is waiting for me to come home, and she'll want me to be in one piece."

"Still can't believe you are married."

"Well, maybe you should try it."

He looks at the road in front of us for a few moments before answering. "I've already tried it. Didn't end well."

I still. I had no idea Sergei was married. "What happened?"

"I killed her." He leans back in the seat and lights a cigarette. "Right after she tried to slice my neck."

"Shit, Sergei."

"Yup. With my own knife. Can you believe that crap?" He blows out a cloud of smoke and focuses on the truck a few yards in front of us.

I look at him and note the dark circles under his eyes. "You aren't sleeping. Again."

"I'll sleep when I'm dead."

The truck gives the right-turn signal and takes the exit. Sergei calls Dimitri.

"He's off the highway and heading your way. ETA seven minutes," he barks, throws the phone on the dash, and leans back in his seat, his mouth widening in a smug smile. "I missed the action, you know?"

I know that smile. We're fucked.

"Fuck!" I jam the crowbar under the truck's cargo doors again and start lifting them up, but the mechanism keeping it from sliding back down doesn't work.

"Sergei! Are you done?"

His voice comes from under the truck. "Just one more."

"You've put enough shit to blow up the whole damn area. Leave it and come here, the door's jammed."

Sergei rolls out from under the truck and comes to my side.

"Just keep it there, I'll get the girl," he says, turns on the flashlight on his phone, and jumps up into the truck.

I hear his footsteps moving further inside, then the sound of boxes being moved.

"Is she there?" I ask.

"I can't find her. Are you sure she's . . . oh, fuck!"

There's some more rustling noises and things being moved.

"Sergei?"

"I've got her. Fuck, she's in a bad shape." His steps come closer. "Hold the door."

I press down on the crowbar, lifting the door higher, then grab the bottom and heft it over my head so Sergei can carry the girl out. Holding a limp female body in his arms, he ducks under the partially raised door and jumps down off the truck. There's no way to see the woman's features, because her tangled hair is all over her face. What I can see are her torn shorts and shirt, and one thin arm hanging limply. She's skin and bones.

"I'll call Varya and tell her to bring the doc." I let the truck door fall back down. "We can meet them at the safe house."

"No. I'm taking her to my place."

"What? Are you crazy?"

"I said I'm taking her with me."

There's a strange look in Sergei's eyes, like he's ready to defend his precious cargo from anyone who'd come close. Roman is going to lose it when he hears about this.

"Whatever. Get her into the car, blow the truck, and let's get out of here."

I call Dimitri on my way to the car and tell him to get the guys and get lost. I expect Sergei to place the girl in the back seat and sit up front, but instead of doing so, he just tightens his arms around her and gets in the back, cradling her. Shaking my head, I start the car and swerve onto the dirt road leading toward the highway.

"Ready?" I look in the rearview mirror and see Sergei staring down at the girl in his arms. "Jesus, Sergei! Get the fucking remote and blow the fucking truck already."

His head snaps up, the eyes narrowed, and he smirks at me. The epic boom pierces the night. My eyes widen. Did he have it on a timer? The bastard could've blown all three of us to pieces if getting the girl had taken a few minutes longer.

I take my phone and call Bruno Scardoni's number.

He answers on the second ring. "What?"

"Dearest Father-in-law." I smile. "The Bratva sends their regards."

I cut the call and dial Roman next. "It's done."

"Everything went as planned?"

"More or less." I sigh.

"Shit. What did he do? It's Sergei, I just know it."

"He wants to take the girl to his place."

"Perfect. Just perfect. Tell him to . . . you know, I don't care. Should I send Varya there?"

"Yes. And the doc. The girl is barely alive."

"Fucking wonderful. I need you here at eight tomorrow morning."

I throw the phone onto the passenger's seat and drive to Sergei's place.

Chapter nineteen

Bianca

I sit up in bed and watch Mikhail getting ready to head to the pakhan's place.

"When will you be back?"

"I don't know." He bends down to kiss me. "I'll message you when I'm done."

"Okay. I'll go wake Lena up. She'll be late."

"You don't have to do that. I'll get her ready."

"I want to. And I style her hair better," I sign and brush his cheek.

When Mikhail leaves, I head into Lena's room, take out the cute pink pants and shirt with matching pink ruffles from her dresser, then go sit next to her on the bed. It takes me two whole minutes of jiggling her nose until she finally wakes up.

"Bianca, Bianca, five more minutes!"

I sigh, remove a few tangled strands of hair from her face, and lean my back against the wall. We can wait five more minutes.

Sisi arrives just as I'm finishing Lena's "many braids"

hairstyle. Lena runs to grab her backpack and heads toward the door, but then she turns and hurries back to me.

"Bianca, Bianca." She leans in and kisses me on the cheek, then runs to join Sisi, waving. "See you later, Mommy."

As I watch her leave, a feeling of warmth spreads inside my chest.

I've just finished showering when my phone rings somewhere. I tense. No one calls me, ever. No point in calling someone over the phone when they can't speak. I run out from the bathroom, rush to the living room, and start looking for my phone. Just as I find it under the throw pillow on the couch, it stops ringing so I check the missed calls and see Allegra's number. Something must have happened if she's calling me. I return the call as I walk back into the bedroom to put some clothes on.

"Bianca," she says the moment the call connects. "I need you to come here right away. Hurry. It's Milene."

The line goes dead, and a feeling of dread collects in my stomach. What's happened to Milene? Why didn't she tell me anything?

I try calling her again, but she doesn't answer, so I throw on the first clothes I find, take my phone and purse, and run out of the apartment. When I get to the sidewalk, I start looking around for a cab, too distracted by all the possibilities of what could've happened to Milene to notice the car that stops right in front of me.

"Bianca!" I hear my father's voice coming from the car. "Let's go."

He opens the passenger door, and without thinking it over, I get inside the car. The sound of doors locking makes my head snap up to glare at my father, who's regarding me with malice in his eyes.

"Cara mia," he sneers, and backhands me with such force I black out.

Mikhail

I'm just parking my car in front of Roman's house when my phone pings with an incoming message. Thinking it must be Bianca, I open the message and my blood goes ice-cold. It's an image of Bianca sitting in an old recliner, hands tied behind her back. She's looking up, probably at the person who took the photo, her face a mask of anger. A big red bruise covers most of her cheek, her lip is split, and a thin line of blood trails down from the corner of her mouth.

The phone in my hand rings, showing Bruno Scardoni's number.

"I'm going to kill you, Bruno," I say the moment I take the call. "I'll make sure it's slow and painful."

"I'll send you the address. You come alone or I'm going to hurt her."

The message with an address somewhere in the suburbs arrives after he ends the call. I drop the car into reverse and floor the gas pedal.

It takes me almost an hour to reach the run-down house

on the outskirts of Chicago. It's a crumbling structure surrounded by overgrown grass and weeds. Two cars are parked next to it, just in front of a door hanging on its hinges. Two men stand on either side it, and another beside one of the cars.

I send a quick message to Denis, instructing him to get here right away, then take my gun from under my seat and head toward the house.

I watch my father as he leans back on the torn couch across from me, holding a gun in his hand. He won't kill me. I know that much. Bruno Scardoni might be an asshole, but he wouldn't kill his own daughter, would he? I have no idea what's going on, but it's evident something's happened. Something big because I have never seen my father in this state. The suit he's wearing is in shambles. His usually carefully slicked-back hair is in disarray, and even though his posture is relaxed, the hand on his knee is trembling slightly as his thumb taps his leg in a fast pattern. I know his tells. He's angry, but based on the look in his eyes, he's also scared.

Not good.

"I had everything planned. It was perfect," he says, looking at the wall behind me. "Every single detail. It was excellent! Pull the Bratva into a war with the Albanians, and then take over their business. The wedding shooter cost me fifty grand, and the idiots who should've killed the son-of-a-bitch husband of yours, a hundred and fifty more. Stupid idiots."

I just stare at him in shock. Our whole family was at the

wedding reception! And I was in the same car with Mikhail when those guys started chasing us, they could have killed us both. Did he even care?

"I was so confident everything would go as planned until your husband blew up my shipment last night. Fifteen million. Gone. The don probably knows already. I'm fucked."

He looks down at me, and a crazy smile spreads across his face. "But I'm not going down alone. I'm going to kill that son of a bitch if it's the last thing I do."

The sound of a car approaching reaches my ears, and my blood runs ice-cold. No. Please God, no. I tug harder on the restraints I've been trying to untie for the past thirty minutes. My right wrist is already raw. I just need to loosen the rope a little bit more and I'll be able to pull out my hand.

A shot rings out in front of the house. Two more follow in quick succession.

"Fucking asshole." My father stands up from the couch and walks toward me.

I lean back in the recliner to hide my hands from his view. He stops on my right and raises his gun to my temple just as Mikhail bursts in through the door. Our gazes collide, and for a moment, all I can do is watch him frozen there, seemingly in perfect control on the outside. His dark blue eye focuses on the gun at my temple.

"Did you kill my men?" my father sneers.

"Yes. Let Bianca go. This is between the two of us, Bruno."

"I don't think so. I think I'd prefer to have her watch. It's all her fault anyway. Isn't it, cara mia?" He looks down at me with such hatred that my breath catches in my lungs.

"You just couldn't, for once in your life, do as I say. I was so thrilled when I heard they'd be marrying you to the Bratva's Butcher. Oh, the plans I had. You know, I wonder . . . do you know why they call him the butcher?"

"Bruno, don't," Mikhail says.

"Oh, you didn't tell her?" My father laughs, grabs my chin with two fingers and turns my head so I'm facing Mikhail again. "Look at your husband, cara. Do you know what he does for the Bratva?"

Mikhail is staring at me, his body tense and his jaw tight, but he doesn't say anything. I already know he's handling the drug's distribution, so I don't understand why he isn't saying anything.

"He tortures people, Bianca. They like to call it an information extraction, but, in reality, it means he beats them, cuts them, and whatever else is needed to make them talk. Look at him well and see the real man you sold your family out for."

I look at Mikhail, willing him to say something, to tell my father he's lying. He doesn't. Instead, he puts his hand in a fist, slowly raises it to his chest, and makes a circular motion, his dark blue eye watching me with sadness the whole time. A sign meaning "*I'm sorry.*"

I close my eyes and take a deep breath. The world we live in is a fucked-up one. I always knew so, and I would be only deceiving myself by believing Mikhail could be anything other than another product of that criminal world. Each item of clothing I own, every meal I've ever eaten has been paid for with blood money. I'm not a hypocrite and will not pretend otherwise. Do I condone violence? No.

Could I torture a person to get the information I needed? Probably not.

I open my eyes and look straight into his blue gaze. Will I love Mikhail less because of what he does? No. A fucked-up world creates fucked-up people. I'm probably one of them, too, because I accept my reality for what it is.

"I love you," I mouth the words to Mikhail and watch him go still as he focuses on my lips.

"My God, you're in love with him," my father says in awe and then bursts out laughing. "But no worries, you're pretty. We'll find you another monster to marry easily enough." He turns to Mikhail. "Take out the magazine and drop the gun."

No, no, no. I watch Mikhail as he releases the magazine and then throws it along with the gun on the floor in front of him.

"There are handcuffs on the radiator in the corner." My father nods toward the other side of the room, still pressing the gun to my head. "Cuff yourself."

Panic rises in my stomach as I watch Mikhail walk toward the radiator, sit on the floor, and put one side of the handcuffs on his right wrist and close the other around the pipe. My father is going to kill him.

"Bruno, please. Let Bianca go. You can do whatever you want with me, but let your daughter go."

"I don't know . . ." He lowers the gun and takes a few steps toward Mikhail. "I think I should let her watch me kill you. Maybe it will make her more reasonable."

Ignoring the searing pain, I pull on my restraints with all my might, rotating my hand left and right. At the same moment when I feel my hand slip free, a gunshot pierces the air. My head snaps up and I watch in horror as blood starts pooling from a wound in Mikhail's shoulder.

"You didn't think I'd let you off easily, did you? I have several more bullets here, and I'll make sure only the last one is fatal." Father takes another step toward Mikhail and cocks his head to the side. "What should I pick next? A leg maybe? Or the other shoulder? You could give me guidelines, it's your specialty."

I spring to my feet and run for Mikhail's gun on the floor near the doorway.

"Bianca!" my father yells. "What the hell do you think you're doing? Leave it alone. You'll hurt yourself, you idiot!"

"Get out and run!" Mikhail shouts at the same time. "Fucking now, Bianca!"

I ignore them both. I'm not running, and I'm certainly going to hurt someone. And it won't be me. I look up at my father, who's standing three yards in front of Mikhail, take the gun in one hand, insert the magazine, and cock the gun. It takes me no more than a few seconds, I've practiced this many times with Angelo. The look in my father's eyes as he watches me stand up and aim the gun at him is priceless.

For a few moments, the two of us just stand there looking at each other, my gun pointed at my father's chest as he regards me.

"You don't have the guts, cara mia." He smiles and starts turning toward Mikhail.

No, I guess I don't have the guts to kill my father. I take a deep breath, aim at his thigh, and pull the trigger.

Bruno Scardoni screams, and his gun falls from his hand. He crumbles to the floor, clutching his bleeding thigh.

I take a couple more steps until I am standing right in front of him.

"That's for me," I rasp, then I aim again—this time at his shoulder—and fire. His body jerks and he falls backward onto the floor. "That's for . . . my husband."

Ignoring my father's weeping, I kick his gun toward the other side of the room.

"Bianca, give me the gun, baby."

I look at Mikhail and his outstretched arm, walk toward him, and put the gun in his free hand.

"Bianca, look at me, solnyshko."

She raises her eyes to mine, and I see she's crying.

"Can I kill him, baby?" I look over at Bruno who's panting on the floor. If Bianca wasn't here, he'd already be dead, but I won't kill him in front of her unless she wants me to.

She shakes her head, then pulls off her T-shirt and squeezes it in a bundle. Crouching in front me in only her bra and jeans, she presses it to my bleeding shoulder. My hand is still cuffed to the radiator pipe, and my shoulder is screaming in pain, but there's no way I'll risk her going near that asshole to find the key. Instead, I wrap my free arm around her and hold her to my chest, making sure the gun in my hand doesn't touch her skin.

The door bangs into the wall and Denis rushes in, gun drawn, looking around.

"Eyes to the floor," I bark. No one is seeing my wife half naked except me, special circumstances be damned.

"The key to the cuffs." I motion with my head toward Bruno. "Tie something around his leg and call Maxim to have someone pick him up and deliver him to the don."

Denis finds the handcuffs keys in one of Bruno's pockets and rushes to unlock the cuffs for me.

"We need to get you to the hospital, Boss," he whispers.

"No. Let's go to Doc's. I'm not going to a hospital with a gunshot wound unless it's necessary. We're taking your car."

"Why it's always my car when transporting vomiting or bleeding passengers?" Denis mumbles while he's calling Maxim.

I place a finger under Bianca's chin and raise her head. "Are you okay, dusha moya?"

She takes my hand and places it on the shirt she's pressing against my shoulder, cups my face with her hands, and kisses me.

"*No. But I will be.*" She signs and kisses me again.

"We need to set up some rules. When I tell you to run, you run, Bianca. Is that clear?"

"*And leave you to be killed?*"

"Yes."

Bruno could have killed her. I didn't think he would, but I'd never risk her life, even if there was a 1 percent possibility she'd end up hurt.

"*I can't promise you that. I'm sorry.*"

"Bianca, baby, if you don't promise me, I'm going to lock you in the apartment and put two men at the door. I'm so angry with you for what you did out there. Please don't test me on this."

"*Okay.*"

"Okay, what? Okay, you promise you'll do as I say?"

She smirks a little, puts her arms around my waist, and places her head on my chest.

I don't know what makes me lift my head from Mikhail's chest and look at my father, lying on the floor a dozen paces or so behind Mikhail. For a moment it looks like he's still passed out, but then my eyes fall to his right hand tucked into his jacket. The scene unfolds as if in slow motion. His hand comes out of his jacket, holding a gun, a mad look in his eyes and a wide smile on his face. He points the gun at Mikhail's back. I step around Mikhail and start to run toward my father. Someone is shouting. One strong arm wraps around my middle, turning me around, my back pressed to Mikhail's wide chest. Two gunshots explode somewhere behind me, almost simultaneously. I feel Mikhail wince and he steps forward, still clutching my body to his. A kiss lands on the top of my head.

"Don't you dare try taking a bullet meant for me ever again," he whispers in my ear.

His arm loosens around me as Denis looks up from my father's unmoving body, then turns and runs toward us. I let out a breath, thankful everything is over and wrap my arms around Mikhail. His shirt is wet. I pull my right palm away—red. Horror builds in my stomach as I look up at Mikhail, who stumbles forward, but Denis manages to catch him.

"Get my car!" Denis shouts, throws Mikhail's arm around his shoulders, and drags him toward the front door. "Now, Bianca!"

I run.

Chapter Twenty

Bianca

I feel someone's hand on my shoulder and open my eyes. Nina is sitting on a chair next to me, watching me.

"Any news?" she asks, but I just shake my head.

They took Mikhail into surgery the moment we arrived at the hospital yesterday. It lasted four hours. The doctor said the bullet nicked his lung, but everything should be okay and they will be releasing him from the ICU today. I was waiting for the nurse to let me know which room they would be moving him to, only to be informed he'd started bleeding internally, and they had to take him into emergency surgery again. That was six hours ago.

"Denis brought some clothes for you," Nina says and reaches for my hand. "A towel and some cosmetics, as well. You need to shower and change. Then, you have to eat something."

I wrap myself in the jacket Denis gave me and shake my head. I'm not leaving this chair until someone comes to tell me Mikhail is okay.

"There's an empty room two doors down. We'll be back in ten minutes, tops. Roman will stay here and call us if anyone comes with news. If Grumpy sees you like this, he'll divorce you straight away, you know that right?"

I look up at the pakhan, who's standing a few feet to my right, and he nods. "I'll be right here and will come get you if the doctor comes out."

I unfold my legs from under me and slowly stand up. I have no idea how many hours I've been in the same position, and my legs feel stiff as if all blood flow to them has ceased. It takes me less than ten minutes to shower, brush my teeth, and put on the jeans and T-shirt I found in the bag. I collect the cosmetics to place them back in the bag when I notice a folded gray hoodie at the bottom. I take it out and start crying again. It's the one I stole from Mikhail. Denis probably packed it thinking it was mine. I'm not cold, but I put it on anyway and return to the waiting room.

Nina looks at me when I enter and smiles, but it doesn't reach her eyes. "Shit, honey. Is that Grumpy's?"

I nod and try to keep the tears from falling again.

Nina sniffs and envelops me into a hug. "He'll be okay, you'll see." She sniffs again. "Come on. Let's find you something to eat."

One hour later the doctor comes out from the operating room and informs us the surgery went well. He tells us to go home and come back in the morning since Mikhail won't be released from ICU before then, but I just shake my head and go back to my seat. I'm not going anywhere.

Across the hallway, Roman and Nina start arguing, but I only catch the part about him threatening to carry her home himself if she doesn't leave. Fifteen minutes later, two men in suits arrive. The older one with glasses approaches Roman and gives him the laptop he brought with him. They sit down at the far end of the hallway, discussing something. The other man follows Nina as she comes to stand in front of me and takes my hand in hers.

"I have to go. Roman threatened to tie me to the bed if I don't go home and get some sleep, but I'm coming back first thing in the morning. If you need anything, message me, okay?"

I squeeze her hand and nod.

"Maxim and Roman will stay with you." She nods to the two of them. "Maxim arranged it with the nurse to let you rest in Mikhail's room until they bring him in. Try to get some sleep."

I don't think I'll manage to do so, but I nod again anyway.

The nurse comes a few minutes after Nina leaves and takes me into the room where I showered earlier. I drop down onto the couch next to the window, take out my phone, and send a message to Sisi asking about Lena. We haven't told her what happened.

I scroll through my phone, going through twenty or so texts from Milene asking about Mikhail and if I need anything. In one, she asks if I'm coming to Father's funeral tomorrow. I let her know Mikhail's condition is unchanged, ignore the funeral part, and throw the phone onto the seat next to me. As far as I'm concerned, I hope my father burns in hell.

The damn vending machine is stuck. I try hitting it with my palm a few times, but nothing happens. Sighing, I leave the machine and head to the cafeteria on the other side of the building. I'm not hungry at all, but I started feeling dizzy in the last hour, probably my body telling me I haven't had any food other than a salad Nina made me eat yesterday.

As I approach the sliding door leading into the cafeteria, I notice my reflection in the glass. My hair is so tangled it looks like I've been assaulted. My face is ghostly pale, except for the dark brown bags under my eyes, and for a second, I debate going inside with all those people there. I look like a train wreck, but then I decide I don't give a damn. I pick the smallest sandwich I can find and a lemonade, and I finish both by the time I get back. As I turn the corner, a nurse exits the room and reaches me in a few strides. I remember her from last night when she came to give me a blanket.

"We've just brought your husband into the room. He's still sedated, but he'll be waking up soon, so just buzz me when he does, okay?"

When I don't say anything, she smiles and lightly squeezes my arm in reassurance. "He'll be fine, sweetheart, don't worry. You should try talking to him, it'll help in waking him up."

Roman and Maxim are standing a few feet down the hallway, watching me. I turn toward the open door only a few steps ahead, but my legs refuse to move any closer. I don't know why, but I'm suddenly afraid to go inside. I take a deep breath, then another, and finally, will my feet to make those few steps and enter the room.

Mikhail is lying with his head tilted to the side, a white sheet covering him up to the chest. There's an IV stand on the side of the bed, and several other tubes and wires. Some of them are attached to a small monitor above, and for a moment, I'm transfixed with the pulsing line showing his heartbeat.

I grab a chair from the corner, place it on the side of the bed and slowly sit down. I want to take his hand and put it to my face, but I'm afraid it'll hurt him, so I just move closer and lay my head on the bed next to his pillow. For some time, I just watch him, hating how still he is, until I gather the courage to reach out and place my palm on his cheek. Someone removed his eye patch. He won't like that.

The nurse said talking would help with waking him up. I'm not sure how good I'll be with doing so, but I'll try my best.

Mikhail

I come awake with a faint sound close to my ear. I try opening my eyes but fail, so I focus on the sound. At first, it's like a vibration in my head, but slowly, it transforms into a voice. It's so weak, barely a whisper, and I need to concentrate to understand the words.

"You scared me . . . so much."

The air smells of a hospital, but I don't know how I got here. My head feels like it's in a fog.

The voice continues whispering, "When you are . . . well enough . . . I'm going . . . to strangle you."

My mind slowly gets back on track, remembering. Going into that house and finding Bruno with his gun pointed at Bianca's head. Bianca running toward her father while he was aiming his gun at me. The panic that consumed me when I realized what was going on. My solnyshko, who tried to come between me and the bullet. I don't know what I would have done if the bullet hit her instead of me.

"I love you . . . please . . .wake up."

The last words get lost. How long has she been talking? I will my eyes to open.

"No more talking," I rasp.

Bianca's head snaps up from my pillow. She leans over me and cups my face with her palms. My vision is blurred, and there's not much light in the room, but I still notice the puffiness and redness around her eyes and the mess her hair is in. I don't remember ever seeing Bianca like this. She sniffs, places a kiss on my mouth, and starts signing, but I can't decipher the shapes her hands make.

"I can't see shit, baby." I sigh and reach for her hand. "Come up here."

She shakes her head, but I pull her toward me. "Come lie next to me. It's okay."

She's reluctant at first, but then carefully climbs up to lie on the edge of the bed and snuggles herself to my side.

"Did you tell Lena what happened?"

I feel the tip of her finger press lightly on my chest, drawing the letters.

N-O

"Good."

The door of the room opens, and Roman comes in. He watches us for a few moments, then approaches the bed.

"What's the damage?" I ask.

"Nicked lung and internal bleeding. They patched you up. Doctor says you should be good as new in a month."

"When can I go home?"

"In two weeks."

I look up at him. "I'm not staying in a hospital for two weeks."

"You'll stay as long as they say you should." Roman barks and points the handle of his cane at me. "And you will do exactly what they tell you to fucking do. That's an order."

"What about work?"

"I'll take over until you are back. You're off the next two months."

He can't be serious. "Two months?"

"Shut the fuck up. You almost got killed," he snarls. "If I catch you working sooner than that, I'm swapping you with Pavel, and you're getting the clubs. You got me, Mikhail?"

I grind my teeth. "Yes, Pakhan."

"Perfect. We're expecting the two of you for dinner when you're better. And use your free time to take your wife on a honeymoon or something. You're not getting a two-month vacation again." He turns to leave, then looks over his shoulder. "Sergei dropped by yesterday when he heard you got shot."

I raise my eyebrows "Here? What for?"

"Yep. Stormed in, asked about you, told me to pass you a message, then left."

"What message?"

"He wants you to text him the list of people who were involved in you getting shot so he can kill them. He said he's free this weekend."

I sigh and shake my head.

I reach out and brush my hand over Mikhail's five-day stubble. It's strange. I've only ever seen him clean-shaven. His scars are much less noticeable with facial hair. He looks different. I look up and find him watching me.

"You like it?" he asks.

I smile and brush my palm over his face again.

"Do you want me to leave it?"

He asks this casually, but he's watching carefully for my reaction. I know what he means. He doesn't like having facial hair, he told me once. But if I say yes, he'll leave it because he thinks I'd prefer his scars hidden. He still doesn't get it. I think he's the most beautiful man I've ever seen.

"*I like it.*" I sign, and he nods, lowering the razor to the sink. "*But I prefer when you are clean-shaven.*"

His hand holding the razor stills.

"Sure?" he asks, and there is doubt in his eye.

I cup his face with my palms, tilt his head down, and kiss him. "I'm sure, Mikhail," I whisper against his lips.

"Okay, baby."

"*Do you want me to do it?*" I've never shaved a man before, but his right arm is in a sling because of his shoulder, and I'm not sure he can manage it only with his left hand. "*I'll be careful. You're going to probably cut yourself.*"

Mikhail just watches me for a few seconds, then laughs. "It's not like it would matter, baby."

I narrow my eyes at him, take his chin between my fingers and squeeze lightly. "*To me, it would matter.*"

"Okay, okay." He smiles, puts down the lid of the toilet, and slowly lowers himself to sit on it. "I'm all yours."

"*Exactly.*" I nod, take the razor and the shaving cream from the sink, then proceed to get my husband back to his original handsome self.

After I am done, I turn to put the shaving supplies back

when I hear the lock on the bathroom door behind me. I turn and find Mikhail smirking at me.

"No," I mouth.

"Yes."

"*You got shot five days ago. Twice. We are not doing anything that requires a locked door.*"

"Come here."

"*No.*"

He reaches forward with his hand, hooks a finger onto the waistband of my jeans, and pulls me toward him until I'm standing between his legs. "Turn around."

I sigh and obey.

"I love when you pretend you're docile." He whispers in my ear and starts unbuttoning my jeans.

I open my mouth to tell him what I think about his declaration since I can't sign to him with my back pressed against his chest, but when his hand slides inside my jeans, the words die on my lips.

"Wet already?" he asks, and I feel his finger entering me. "I like that. I like that very much, Bianca."

He bites my shoulder and adds another finger, making me gasp.

"What do you think, how much time will it take me to make you come, hmm?" He makes a slow circling motion around my clit. "Five minutes?"

I close my eyes and nod my head.

"I doubt it, baby." He whispers, then pinches my clit lightly. "You won't last more than two minutes."

I lean back onto his chest and open my legs slightly wider. The things this man can do with his hand . . . it's crazy.

"Eyes, Bianca."

I open them and watch our reflections in the mirror above the sink—Mikhail's hand between my legs and a wolfish smile on his face. He removes his finger and I want to scream, but then he thrusts it back all the way in and presses my clit with his thumb, and I shatter instantly.

"Barely a minute and a half, baby." He kisses my shoulder. "We'll try again later. See if we can make it in under a minute."

Wicked, wicked man.

EPILOGUE

Six weeks later

Bianca

"I *HAVE A SURPRISE FOR YOU*." I SIGN AND PLACE MY hands on Mikhail's chest.

"Oh? What is it?"

I let my lips widen in a smug smile, take a hold of his tie, and take a step backward, pulling him toward me. Mikhail's eyebrow lifts, but he follows me, taking one step forward for every two of mine as he allows me to lead him across the living room to the gym. Without letting go of his tie, I turn the knob and drag him inside, waiting for his reaction when he sees the setup I've prepared. He stops at the threshold to look at the blinds I pulled all the way down over the floor-to-ceiling windows. The only light in the room is from the two lamps I moved from the living room and placed in opposing corners. His lips lift when he spots the chair I've placed in the middle of the room, but he doesn't comment. Curling my finger at him, I draw him into my makeshift theater, leading him until we reach the chair.

"*Sit down,*" I sign and push lightly at his chest.

Mikhail lowers himself to the chair and cocks his head to the side, pursing his lips as if trying to read my intentions.

"*Close your eyes. And no peeking.*"

"All right." He smiles and leans back in the chair.

I place a light kiss on his lips, then rush toward the corner, where I left my tulle skirt and ballet slippers hidden under a towel. It takes me less than two minutes to get out of my dress and put on the slippers, cropped top, and skirt. At first, I planned on wearing a leotard but it would get in the way later. After debating for a few seconds, I take off my panties and throw them over the discarded dress. With a glance over my shoulder at Mikhail, I smile in anticipation as I set the PA system to play at max volume. In the pause I included before my playlist begins, I assume an open fourth position with one arm outstretched in a soft arc.

The opening sounds of Chopin's "Nocturne No.9" fill the room, and Mikhail's eye snaps open. I smile, blow him a kiss, and begin. I draw myself into a pirouette, slowly extend my leg in a suspended *developpé,* my opening sequence from *Swan Lake,* then continue into a series of different types of choreography. Mikhail's eye watches me without blinking, following my every move. I've grown accustomed to men looking at me, both on stage and off, but no one has ever looked at me the way Mikhail does. Like I am something precious, and he's afraid that if he moves his eye from me, I might disappear. Such a silly man, my husband. No one will make me let go of him. Ever. I perform an *arabesque* and a few smaller steps until I am standing right in front of him. Then do a *fouetté*, just to make sure he notices I'm not wearing panties, and stop at the same moment when the Chopin piece ends.

There are a few seconds of silence, during which he just watches me with a small smile on his lips. He probably thinks this was all I've prepared, and when the sound of John Legend's "All of Me" fills the room, he quirks his eyebrow. I smile and step forward, coming to stand between his legs. The first verse passes with us staring at each other without even touching, but when the choir sings, I place my left palm over his right cheek and, without breaking eye contact, remove his eyepatch with my free hand.

"All of me," I whisper and place a kiss on his lips. "All of you . . . baby."

He regards me as his hand comes to the back of my neck, threading my hair through his fingers and squeezing. I remove his tie and unbutton his shirt. Mikhail doesn't say a word, only watches me while his grip on my hair keeps my head unmoving. It's as if he wants to keep my face in sight.

When the chorus starts again, I remove his shirt and bend to press my lips over his scarred right eyelid. "All your . . . imperfections."

He takes a deep breath and cups my face between his huge rough palms, his touch so impossibly tender. I smile and, with my finger, trace a heart shape on his chest.

I can't believe I almost lost him. The nightmares of that day still plague me, and I wake up in the middle of the night with panic squeezing my chest. Leaning forward, I slam my lips against his while my hands travel to his bare back, heedless of his older scars. But when I feel the raised round mark under my fingers, I shudder and squeeze him tighter to me.

Mikhail

There's not much light in the room, but, even with my slightly blurred vision, I can see the tears gathering in the corners of Bianca's eyes.

"Baby? What's wrong?"

She presses her lips together and touches her forehead to mine while her finger traces a pattern around the already healed gunshot wound on my back.

"Bianca, look at me, baby."

She lifts her head, and I take her chin between my fingers. "I'm okay. Can you please try to forget about it?"

Her hand rests at the nape of my neck and she nods, but I know she's lying because one tear escapes and rolls down her cheek. I can't take it. For years, I believed there was nothing I couldn't endure, but seeing Bianca cry because of me . . . I can't take that.

"Do you want me to reassure you, my little lamb?" I ask as I trail my hand down the center of her chest and stomach, then reach under her tulle skirt to press my fingers at her pussy.

She takes a deep breath and nods, and I slide my finger inside her. Standing up from the chair, I start unbuttoning my pants with my right hand, without removing the left one from her pussy. When I manage to get rid of my pants, I take the waistband of her skirt and pull it up and over her head, then turn her around and press her back to me, wrapping my free hand around her waist.

"Ready?" I ask and nuzzle her neck.

She nods, and I tighten the arm around her, then lift her

and head out of the gym. Bianca squeezes my forearm and presses her legs together, panting as I carry her. I make sure I go slow, teasing the inside of her all the way to the bedroom, and by the time we reach the bed, she's already close to coming.

"Not yet, baby." I set her down next to the bed and slowly remove my finger from her, but instead of lying down, she climbs to stand on the edge of the bed and presses her palms onto my chest.

"I want to . . ." she whispers, "tell you . . . so much."

"You don't have to say anything, Bianca." I press my lips to hers, then slide my palms down her back and grab her under her ass. I planned on savoring her in the bed but have changed my mind, so I pull her up until her legs wrap around my waist and I turn to lean her back against the wall. I lower her onto my rock-hard cock slowly, loving the way her breath catches when I fill her up.

"Even half blind, I can see everything, baby." I slide out and then slam into her. "Every." Slam. "Single." Slam. "Thing."

Bianca whimpers, squeezing her arms around my neck as she inhales to the beat of me pounding into her. She usually closes her eyes when she comes, but this time, she keeps them wide open, holding my gaze as she trembles and pants. I explode inside her like never before, then crash my mouth to hers, squeezing her body to mine and holding her long after we both come down from the high.

Shit. Something isn't right.

I try working the dough a bit more, but it's still sticking

to my fingers. After wiping the flour from my hands on the apron, I take the phone from the back pocket of my jeans and open the message window. I promised Lena piroshki for dinner, and I need to make this dough right, damn it.

19:22 Bianca: I've fucked up something, the dough looks like bubble gum. Can you check with Igor to see if he gave you the right measurements?

19:24 Nina: Just try adding more flour. He gives me different measurements every time I ask and I'm starting to wonder if he's doing it on purpose. Doesn't want anyone to get his piroshki recipe probably. I'll tell Roman to scare him a bit, maybe he'll succumb then.

19:25 Bianca: Please don't. Lol. I'll try adding more flour. Anything new there?

19:26 Nina: Roman just came back from Sergei's place. He said the house looks like a hurricane went through it. Sergei smashed everything.

19:27 Bianca: Why? I've never met the guy, but from what I heard from Mikhail, he's a little . . . unhinged.

19:29 Nina: That's an understatement of the century, dear. Looks like the girl he had at his place disappeared and he went ballistic. Want to come over?

I'm just typing my answer when I feel a light touch at the base of my neck, followed by a kiss.

"Dusha moya . . ."

I smile and start to turn around, but Mikhail winds his arm around my waist and keeps my back pressed to his chest. He nuzzles my neck as his right hand comes to rest on the countertop in front of me, holding a single yellow rose. All the breath leaves my lungs as I stare at the delicate flower, its stem wrapped in a wide yellow silk ribbon embroidered with gold.

"I never told you," he whispers in my ear, "that I was always your biggest fan. I still am."

"Mikhail?" I utter, my eyes still focused on the flower.

"There was a poster I saw one evening—I think it was in a shop window—almost a year ago. I remember walking past it, and then retracing my steps to take a better look at the image. It showed a group of dancers. All except one were wearing yellow costumes, and as I regarded them, I wondered why, among all of them, the one dancer who wore a black outfit shined brighter than the rest." A kiss lands at the side of my neck. "Like a sun."

He turns me to face him then, cups my face with his hand, and places a soft kiss on my lips. "I never missed any of your shows after that. I love you, my little sun. My solnyshko."

I wind my arms around his waist and bury my face in his chest. "I love you, too . . . my Mikhail."

Dear reader,

Thanks so much for reading! I hope you'll consider leaving a review, letting the other readers know what you thought of Broken Whispers. Even if it's one short sentence, it makes huge difference. Reviews help authors find new readers, and help other readers find new books to love!

Neva Altaj writes steamy contemporary mafia romance about damaged antiheroes and strong heroines who fall for them. She has a soft spot for crazy jealous, possessive alphas who are willing to burn the world to the ground for their woman. Her stories are full of heat and unexpected turns, and a happily-ever-after is guaranteed every time.

Neva loves to hear from her readers,
so feel free to reach out:

Website: www.neva-altaj.com

Facebook: www.facebook.com/neva.altaj

TikTok: www.tiktok.com/@author_neva_altaj

Instagram: www.instagram.com/neva_altaj

Amazon Author Page: www.amazon.com/Neva-Altaj

Goodreads: www.goodreads.com/Neva_Altaj

BookBub:www.bookbub.com/authors/neva-altaj